X-COUNTRY ADVENTURES

Mystery in Massachusetts

Bob Schaller

A Division of Baker Book House Co
Grand Rapids, Michigan 49516

Books in the X-Country Adventure series

Message in Montana
South Dakota Treaty Search
Adventure in Wyoming
Crime in a Colorado Cave
Mystery in Massachusetts

Published by Baker Books
a division of Baker Book House Company
P.O. Box 6287, Grand Rapids, MI 49516-6287

Printed in the United States of America

Library of Congress Cataloging-in-Publication Data

Schaller, Bob.
Mystery in Massachusetts / Bob Schaller.
p. cm. (X-country adventures)
Summary: Ashley and Adam Arlington reveal pieces of their puzzle as they follow a scavenger hunt along the Freedom Trail through Boston to Bunker Hill.
ISBN 0-8010-4491-X (paper)
[1. Treasure hunts—Fiction. 2. Brothers and sisters—Fiction. 3. Boston (Mass.)—Fiction. 4. Mystery and detective stories.] I. Title
PZ7.S33366 My 2001
[Fic]—dc21 2001043025

For current information about all releases from Baker Book House, visit our web site:

http://www.bakerbooks.com

Contents

A Beginning and an End

Adam and Ashley Arlington could hardly contain their excitement. "It's just your competitive side," Ashley told her sixteen-year-old brother. "You want to win."

"Hey, Sis," Adam answered his seventeen-year-old sibling, "I see a smile on your face that reaches both ears. Don't tell me you're not excited about this!"

"This" was a scavenger hunt for everyone who participated in a summer leadership camp just outside of Boston. Those staying around the area upon the camp's conclusion were invited to participate, with parental approval. While there hadn't been a large group of kids whose families were staying around Boston, Adam and Ashley figured close to a dozen kids planned to coax their parents into it out of the twenty-five at that week's camp session.

"You think Mom and Dad will go for this?" Adam asked his sister.

"To learn about history and see the sites in Boston?" Ashley asked rhetorically. "I think so!"

Their mother was a history professor at a college near their home in Washington, D.C., so the kids knew they never had to ask twice when they wanted to do any activity that involved history and learning lessons from the past. Their parents were due to pick them up within the hour at the leadership camp's headquarters, and Ashley didn't expect to have any trouble talking her mom and dad into staying on to participate in the special scavenger hunt.

Adam and Ashley unfolded the camp's brochure, map, and directions for the scavenger hunt, which was titled *Why Freedom Rings*.

"This is quite a list," Ashley said. "The scavenger hunt goes along the Freedom Trail, which has sixteen stops."

The kids knew a bit about Boston's famous Freedom Trail, a two-and-a-half-mile outdoor walking trail that passes by several historical landmarks, including the Boston Massacre site and Paul Revere's House.

Adam read from the scavenger hunt sheet. "This list includes everything from boats to books. 'Must be completed by the evening of July 3, at the boat.' I wonder why it says that?"

"The Fourth of July is the next day," Ashley reminded him. "Maybe the holiday plays into it somehow."

"Good point," Adam said. "But this list doesn't tell us where to find these things along the Freedom Trail. How are we supposed to know where to start?"

Ashley shrugged her shoulders. "Maybe there will be more clues that will give us a starting point at the informational meeting tonight. We're supposed to meet at the Bunker Hill Monument at 6:00."

The warm morning breeze started to blow a bit as their parents pulled up in the family's SUV just before 9:30. As Adam and Ashley picked up their bags, their parents, Anne and Alex, came over and hugged them.

"Long time no see," Mr. Arlington said.

"Dad," Ashley said, rolling her eyes, "it's only been five days!"

"You know your father," Mrs. Arlington said with a smile. "He'll want a complete recap."

As a prominent lawyer, Alex Arlington always asked questions until he knew the facts of any case—all the facts. Sometimes he questioned his teens the same way, which occasionally made them groan and say, "Dad, you're being a lawyer again!" Usually, though, they answered his questions patiently, and his inquiring mind had often led them into some interesting family discussions.

"Meet, eat, sleep. Meet, eat, sleep," Adam told his father, drawing laughs. "Only two of the kids were from Boston, and guess what? They're headed to our hometown, Washington, D.C., tomorrow. So the only kids in the scavenger hunt would be out-of-towners, like us."

"What scavenger hunt?" asked Mr. Arlington.

The kids piled into the car and immediately talked to their parents about the scavenger hunt. Ashley read the brochure as her parents listened.

"There's a meeting tonight at 6:00 at the Bunker Hill Monument," Ashley said. "Can we go?"

Mr. and Mrs. Arlington looked at each other. They had planned a trip to Cape Cod for the next night, to last through the end of the family's vacation. But the excitement in their children's voices—plus the opportunity to work in a bit more history and sight-seeing in the final week of their vacation—sounded too good to pass up.

"I think we can fit that in," their mother said as their father nodded in agreement. "But we are planning to head to Cape Cod tomorrow night. So if this is more than a one-day thing, I don't know that we'll be able to do it."

"I thought we're supposed to always finish what we start," Adam said, reminding his parents of their often-used saying.

"Good point," Mr. Arlington said. "But we've made reservations for this Cape Cod trip. You know we have friends from college there that we'd like to have time to visit. So if we can't fit in the scavenger hunt, we simply won't start it. Is that a more clear answer?"

"Yes, Dad," Adam said. "I'm sorry. I'm just really excited about this. Can we at least see what it involves, though, before we shoot it down?"

"We most certainly can," Mrs. Arlington said. "After all, we do have some spare time."

The vacation was to end in four days, and the trip back to the family's home in Washington, D.C. wouldn't be as long as it had been during some of their past trips, especially to the Midwest. Mr. and Mrs. Arlington figured they might as well soak in as much of history-rich Boston as they could now with their kids. First, though, they wanted to hear more about the leadership camp.

"All right, aside from the meeting, eating, and sleeping, what did you do at camp?" Mrs. Arlington asked.

Ashley nodded toward Adam, prompting him to answer first. "We talked a lot about what leadership is," Adam said. "We learned that leaders set an example. Our leadership 'coach' talked about how the best leaders are the ones who work the hardest and complain the least. We also learned that most good leaders are organized in their actions and their thoughts. And a good leader doesn't usually make rash decisions."

Their mom winked at their dad. Neither parent was surprised that those aspects of leadership had stood out in their son's mind. Adam had shown that he could take action when he needed to—he was a leader on Thomas Jefferson High School's winning track team, and he knew how to lead a pack. Sometimes when he was excited about something he could even be impulsive and act too quickly. Most of the time, though, he preferred to organize his thoughts and plan out his actions in advance. Adam's favorite thing to do in his free time was use his laptop to go online and research whatever he was interested in at the moment. He usually liked to consider things from every angle before deciding what to do.

"So once a leader is prepared, is he or she always out front setting the pace?" Mrs. Arlington asked.

Ashley shook her head. "No way," she answered. "A leader isn't afraid to be at the back of the pack, picking up those who are struggling or helping someone with a task where they need direction."

"That sounds like a good quality for everyone to have," her mom said. "I'm impressed with what you've learned. What was the highlight of the week, do you think?"

Ashley thought for a minute. "The thing that made the biggest impression on me is that a leader doesn't have to sing her own praises. A leader lets her actions speak for her.

"One of our activities was to divide into groups, appoint a leader, and take an overnight camping trip. We had to use a map and compass to find food and water supplies put out ahead of time by the camp staff, and we had to find a good area on our own to make a cook fire, set up our tents, and spend the night. The staff was keeping an eye on us, but they wanted to see if we could make it on our own under our group leader.

"There was one guy who put together his entire team's camping project—well, at least the trickiest parts of it. He went on and on pointing out his contributions to his group's 'survival.' If he had let his work speak for itself, he would've gotten a lot more respect, I think.

"On the other hand, our camping group had a girl leader who did some of the bigger tasks. But she quietly helped everyone with what they were doing too. She didn't seek out any credit. In fact, when they asked our group to sum up how the project went, she didn't say a word. And sure enough, the rest of us talked about how good she was at keeping our team on the right path. Was she as experienced a camper as the guy in the other group? I don't know, maybe—or maybe not. But she was definitely a better leader. Everyone really respected her."

"Interesting," Mr. Arlington said.

"Yeah," Adam added. "She didn't put down the people in our group who didn't understand things like how to set up a tent so it would *stay* up, like the guy in the other group did. You don't have to be 'loved' to be a good leader, but it sure helps to be liked. And, of course, a leader earns respect. Being able to figure out everyone's strengths and weaknesses is an important part of being a leader too. The girl who led our camping group—her name is Rachel Dunn—really got our whole team working together. We were all smiling when we completed our task—especially when the tents finally stayed up. Nobody in the other guy's group looked too happy when they were done from what we could see, even though they completed the same task in probably the same amount of time."

The Arlingtons were glad their teens had learned a lot from their experience at leadership camp. They were also glad Ashley had gained some experience in the camping group with another girl her age who knew how to lead quietly behind the scenes. Tall and blonde, Ashley was a star player on TJHS's girls' volleyball and basketball teams, and she excelled in her studies, especially in the school's chemistry club. Her strong point, though, was helping other kids excel, too, rather than being the one out in front of the group all the time. She was a "team player."

"Did you and your camping group leader, Rachel, have a lot in common?" her mother asked her.

"Some things," Ashley answered. "Rachel isn't into her school sports program like I am, but she's still involved in leading things, like being an editor of her school newspaper. And I don't think her family has gone camping much like we have. When she had problems with our tents, though, instead of trying to take charge and acting like she knew everything, she asked us to take over that part. She wasn't afraid to learn from people under her or help them do what they did best. I liked that about her."

"She has a brother a year younger than me, too," Adam added. "His name is Ryan, and he was in the other guy's camping group. He was making lots of faces at his sister from across the clearing, but I think by the end of the night he was really wishing he was over in her group with us!"

Mr. and Mrs. Arlington laughed at that.

"So he might have thought that being in a group whose leader can share the responsibility *and* the praise would be better than being in a show-off leader's group, even if it meant following his own sister's orders?" Mrs. Arlington asked.

"I guess so," said Adam, "though if I were him I would have wanted to stay in the show-off's group anyway—at least during camp. His sister probably bosses him around enough at home!"

Ashley gave her brother a not-so-playful punch on the shoulder for that wisecrack. Adam quickly returned one of his own, and Mr. and Mrs. Arlington decided it might be a good time to park the car and do some walking.

After getting into downtown Boston, the family parked and rode the "T" subway to Quincy Market, spending the day shopping, snacking, and discussing more details about the leadership camp.

"Let's go see Boston Common," Mrs. Arlington said, noticing a sign that promoted the historic route.

"Not yet!" Adam said. "That could be part of the scavenger hunt!"

"Oh yes, the hunt," she replied with a smile. "Hey, it's almost 5:00. Who's ready to head back to the car and to the Bunker Hill Monument? And don't forget, Bunker Hill itself is part of the Freedom Trail."

She didn't wait for an answer. She didn't have to—Ashley and Adam were already turned and in full sprint heading toward the subway.

"If their excitement is contagious," Mr. Arlington said, "it looks like you and I'd better be up for some running."

His wife smiled, starting off ahead of her husband and just behind Adam and Ashley.

After catching the "T" and getting back to their SUV, the Arlingtons arrived at Bunker Hill at 5:45.

"Fifteen minutes early," Adam said proudly. Their parents always preached the importance of not being late.

There were ten families gathered for the meeting about the scavenger hunt. Adam and Ashley greeted several friends they had made at the leadership camp, then they introduced their parents to Rachel and Ryan Dunn. The Dunns were also staying to take part in the scavenger hunt, and their parents, Lawrence and Kathleen, stood chatting with Mr. and Mrs. Arlington. The four kids read the information around the Bunker Hill Monument and talked some more about camp, wondering where the camp leaders were who were supposed to be organizing the scavenger hunt. The families waited for forty-five minutes, but no one showed up to run the scavenger hunt.

About an hour after everyone arrived, a harried man in a gray suit walked up carrying a briefcase.

"There's been a problem," said the man, who introduced himself as Jason Jackson, a staff representative the kids all recognized from the leadership camp. "A donor who wished to remain anonymous contacted our camp through a third party several months ago about setting up this scavenger hunt for our Fourth of July week graduates—your group. This out-of-town donor prepared the packets for the hunt and promised a special Independence Day reward for the first ones in your group to get to the end of it. However, he or she never provided the camp with a name, nor with a description of what the reward actually is or where to find it along the Freedom Trail.

"The local third-party person was supposed to set up all the information and clues along the trail and help us guide the hunt. Unfortunately, this contact person has had a death in the family and has been called away from Boston just as we were supposed to begin the hunt. He left in such a hurry that he barely had time to call us at camp and notify us that he had to leave town. He did say that the prize was in place, but that he couldn't take the time to go back and make sure all the clues were in place on the trail, and that he'd do his best to come back at some point in the future to try to wrap up the details. He left no forwarding phone number or address. Of course you can understand that this would be no time to contact him anyway, during a family member's funeral.

"I apologize to everyone here, but it looks like the scavenger hunt is off. I have no idea whether the organizations or historic sites that were to be included in this hunt have been contacted or if the material for the hunt was actually delivered to them," Jackson said. "Under the circumstances, moving forward with the organized hunt would be of little purpose. The camp staff feel we should wait for further contact from this third party, then proceed with the hunt at another time," he announced. "Right now there may be important clues missing along the way, and there is no way to be sure that we could bring the hunt to a satisfying conclusion and find the reward."

There was a collective groan from the group of families.

"So I guess," Jackson concluded, "the scavenger hunt is canceled."

An End and a Beginning?

"Canceled!" exclaimed Adam. "They can't do that."

"Well, they have," Mrs. Arlington said, putting her arm around her son's shoulder and consoling him.

"Mr. Jackson," Mr. Arlington said as the group turned to look at him. "Is there any way this hunt can go forward? You did mention that the reward is a special Independence Day prize. If the hunt doesn't go forward this week, the holiday will be over. It would be a whole year before the appropriate time for this kind of scavenger hunt comes again. Also, if the contact person 'couldn't take the time to go back and make sure all the clues were in place,' that must mean that at least some of the clues are already out there, if he was just going back to check on them . . ."

Even though his audience wasn't in a courtroom, Mr. Arlington was stating his best case, using all his lawyer's powers of persuasion, for the scavenger hunt to go forward.

Mr. Jackson, however, couldn't give his approval on behalf of the leadership camp.

"You have some good points," he conceded. "I wish it could go forward this week, but I'm afraid I have no information other than what is in these packets. Anyone here is certainly welcome to the information. You can see for yourself what little there is to go on. If you would like to pursue the hunt along the Freedom Trail on your own, I have no objection. You might not get very far, though. And I need to make it clear that the hunt can no longer be associated in any way with the leadership camp, due to insurance and liability concerns. We won't have a staff member available to help with it, nor do we have any further information to provide you with, other than what you see here.

"I would ask one favor of you, however. If any of you do pursue this on your own and you come up with anything, would you notify the camp so that we know what's out there and where we stand? We've been left with a lot of loose ends here. I'm sorry to disappoint you all, and I apologize again. I do want to thank you for being a part of our leadership camp, though. We had a great time with your group and hope to see some of you again in the future!"

With that, Jackson bid farewell and headed away from Bunker Hill.

Most of the families also started to leave, with several of the kids coming over to Ashley and Adam to say goodbye. Soon only the Arlingtons and the Dunns remained.

"Let's see what else is in the packet Mr. Jackson left us." Ashley said.

"Well, maybe it is something worthwhile, maybe not—but there's only one way to find out," Mrs. Arlington said.

The Arlingtons and the Dunns were the only families who had picked up packets from Mr. Jackson before he had gone back to camp. The folders were a patriotic red, white, and blue. Inside each folder were just two sheets of paper. The cover letter was brief and to the point. It was on plain white paper with no letterhead.

"Go in order," Ashley read from the cover sheet. "Cut no corners. And while you will look forward on the trail as you proceed, don't forget that the water might hold an answer as you cross the finish line. Things aren't always as they a pier, and that thought should boat well. Don't break the chain . . . the quest ends on a chain."

Ashley noticed the typos. "They spelled appear like this: A P-I-E-R," she said. "And I think 'boat well' is supposed to be 'bode well.' Or at least that would seem to make sense."

Beneath those instructions was something titled *A Walk through Time*. Ashley read it out loud for the two families:

1630 Puritans establish the town of Boston.

1670 The first Old South Meeting House, a two-story cedar hall, is built.

1761 James Otis speaks against the Writs of Assistance at the Old State House.

1764 The Sugar Act taxation and Currency Act infuriate colonists.

1765 The Stamp Act taxation sparks rioting in Boston.

1768 September 18—British garrison troops in Boston.

1770 March 5—The Boston Massacre leaves five patriots dead. British uphold the Tea Act.

1773 December 16—The Boston Tea Party prompts the Intolerable Acts as punishment.

1775 April 18—Paul Revere and William Dawes Jr. ride from Boston to alert the countryside that British troops are headed to Lexington.

1775 April 19—The British retreat to Boston after the Battles of Lexington and Concord.

1775 June 17—The Battle of Bunker Hill leaves heavy casualties.

1776 March 17—George Washington liberates Boston. British evacuate with troops and local Tories.

1776 July 18—Declaration of Independence is read from the Old State House balcony.

1788 June 21—The Constitution is ratified.

1789 George Washington makes triumphal visit to Boston as first president.

1795 Construction begins for the new State House.

1797 October 21—USS *Constitution* is launched.

1809 The Park Street Church is built.

1822 Boston is incorporated as a city.

1829 July 4—William Lloyd Garrison speaks against slavery at the Park Street Church.

1843 June 17—Bunker Hill Monument is dedicated.

The Arlingtons and Dunns passed the papers around to study.

"Bizarre," Mr. Arlington said. "That's very informational, but it's nothing one wouldn't find in a history book. I'm not sure this makes enough sense to continue the hunt on our own."

There was also a piece of parchment paper in the packet. It appeared to describe some colonial history.

"Here," Rachel Dunn said, tossing her long, black hair over her shoulder. "I'll read it."

She began: "After the French and Indian War, Britain needed a new imperial design, but the situation in America was anything but favorable to change. Long accustomed to a large measure of independence, the colonies were demanding more freedom. To tighten control, Parliament had to contend with colonists trained in self-government who didn't like British interference.

"One of the first things the British tried was to restrict the colonists' movement into the interior. Needing more land for settlement, various colonies wanted to extend their boundaries as far west as the Mississippi River. Britain feared this would provoke a series of Indian wars. The Royal Proclamation of 1763 reserved all the western territory between the Alleghenies, Florida, the Mississippi River, and Quebec for use by Native Americans. Thus the Crown attempted to stop westward expansion. Though never effectively enforced, this measure, in the eyes of the colonists, constituted a high-handed disregard for their most elementary right to occupy and settle western lands.

"More serious was the new financial policy of the British government, which needed more money to support its growing empire. Unless the taxpayer in England was to supply all money for the colonies' defense, revenues would have to be extracted from the colonists themselves. The

Molasses Act of 1733 and the Sugar Act of 1764 caused consternation among New England merchants. Merchants, legislatures, and town meetings protested, and colonial lawyers found in the preamble of the Sugar Act the first intimation of 'taxation without representation,' the slogan that was to draw many to the American cause against the mother country.

"Later in 1764, Parliament enacted a Currency Act 'to prevent paper bills of credit hereafter issued in any of His Majesty's colonies from being made legal tender.' Since the colonies were a deficit trade area and were constantly short of hard currency, this measure added a serious burden to the colonial economy. Equally objectionable from the colonial viewpoint was the Quartering Act, passed in 1765, which required colonies to provide royal troops with provisions and barracks."

Rachel took a deep breath after the long reading. "That's a great history lesson, but I'm not sure what it has to do with the scavenger hunt, other than being part of Boston's history," she said, puzzled.

"There certainly isn't much to go hunting on here," Mr. Dunn commented, "but Kathleen and I have always liked Boston, and we wanted to bring the kids sight-seeing here anyway after their week at camp. We may give this a try just to see where it leads, and if it leads to nothing more than a tour around the Freedom Trail, well, that's what we're here for anyway."

His short, dark-haired wife agreed. "I think the misspellings with 'A P-I-E-R' for appear and 'boat well' for bode well are pretty good clues about where the hunt would end, especially combined with the part in the note that says 'don't forget that the water might hold an answer as you cross the finish line.' So we know where this thing probably ends; it's just a matter of getting from here to there. We'd have to figure out where to get started, or we could end up all washed up . . ."

Everyone laughed at that, but Rachel and Ryan told their parents they thought it would be fun to take on the challenge anyway, since they were going to be in Boston for a few more days.

Mr. Dunn turned to the Arlingtons. "So what do you think?" he asked. "Are you going to stay in Boston long enough to scavenge for some clues? There are four of us and four of you—we could make a race of it and still have a contest!"

All four kids' eyes lit up when they heard Mr. Dunn's proposal, and they noisily agreed to the challenge. For Ashley and Adam, however, the excitement was short-lived when they saw the hesitation on their parents' faces. It looked like for them the scavenger hunt was really off after all . . .

"It would really take something to get us to put time and energy into this thing," Mrs. Arlington said. Her husband nodded his head in agreement.

As their faces fell, she could see that both her kids and the Dunn kids were disappointed by her words.

She went on to explain to both families, "I mean, I'm really searching for some kind of sign that this is how we should spend the last few vacation days we have, especially since we already have other plans in place that don't hinge on an anonymous donor and an out-of-town contact person."

Last Name, First Clue

"Look on the back of the cover letter you're holding," Adam said to his sister, taking the white paper from her. He flipped the page over so everyone could see it and read the big, black letters running across the paper: "ARLINGTON!" he exclaimed. "How's that for a sign?"

The Arlingtons and Dunns laughed.

"That's an awfully good sign, I admit," said Mrs. Arlington. "What else does it say?"

Adam read out loud:

Now you know your **A-B-Cs**—
B-C starts the Freedom Trail,
But before **B-C** you must stop at **A:** "**A**"rlington.
Old Schwab Mill . . . there "wood" be
an answer there that rings a bell.

"I can certainly appreciate the 'Arlington' reference," Mrs. Arlington smiled, "and that does appeal to our sense of curiosity. At the same time, though . . ."

"Oh, Mom!" Adam and Ashley pleaded in unison.

Mr. Arlington too looked at his wife the same way, as if to support the kids' eagerness despite the long odds that anything would materialize from the hunt, except possibly disappointment.

"All right! All right!" she said. "I suppose that we're heading to Arlington first thing in the morning."

Cheers from both families greeted her announcement.

"You won't be sorry, Mom," Adam said. "This is going to be fun no matter how it ends!"

"Right on!" Ryan Dunn said, slapping a high five to Adam. Ryan's fiery enthusiasm matched the fiery color of his hair. In contrast to the smaller, dark-featured Mrs. Dunn and Rachel, Ryan copied the features of his father. He and Mr. Dunn were both tall and big framed, with red hair and flashing green eyes. Mr. Dunn even had a thick, curly red beard that made him look fierce, although he was known for his gentleness. But there was nothing gentle about his son's excitement at the moment.

"This is going to be terrific!" shouted Ryan. "How about if we trade people too? Adam and I could be on one team with Dad and Mr. Arlington, then the girls and moms could be on the other team. It could be guys against the girls, and we'd beat them for sure!"

"Hold on," Mr. Dunn said. "That's not a bad idea, except that this is supposed to be a *family* vacation from here on out. You've been with Adam and Ashley at camp this week, and I can see you all became friends, but we've missed you, and I'm sure Mr. and Mrs. Arlington feel the same way. Plus this scavenger hunt could take some time, and there are the issues of different hotel rooms and riding together and not all being in the same place at the same time. If the Arlingtons agree, I think we'll make this a competition between the two families to keep it simple. Under the circumstances, the hunt will already be challenging enough.

"What do you think?" he asked the Arlingtons.

"Well, Ryan's suggestion might have been fun if we were all in familiar territory, but you're probably right. It will be easier this time to stay with our families," Mr. Arlington replied. "I think, though, that since the historic sites are closed for the evening, we'd be open to hitting a restaurant with you so the kids could have some more time together tonight. What do you say to that, Ryan?" he asked.

"Great!" Ryan answered. "A guys-versus-girls scavenger hunt would have been more fun, but having pizza together would help me get over the disappointment!"

Everyone laughed at that.

"He was complaining the whole time at camp about how their dinners couldn't get an extra-cheese pepperoni pizza off his mind," Rachel told her parents.

"That's one wish of yours we can take care of right now," Mrs. Dunn told Ryan. "I've got a taste for one of those myself! And while we eat, we can set up some of the ground rules for the hunt," she finished.

The two families headed to a nearby restaurant. After some time spent eating and getting to know each other better, they talked about how to proceed with the scavenger hunt.

"We know we need to start in Arlington," Mrs. Arlington said. "If it weren't for that coincidence with our last name, we might not still be here," she smiled. "After that, it looks like the best course would be to start at **B-C**—Boston Common maybe?—on the Freedom Trail, like the cover letter's clue said, and inquire at each of the sixteen historical sites along the way. Mr. Jackson didn't know whether the contact person had finished arranging all the clues along the route for us, so my guess is that some of the guides who work at the sites may be familiar with the camp's plans for the scavenger hunt, and others may have no idea about it. We'll just have to see as we go along."

"That's right," Mr. Arlington agreed. "I think we'll head back to our hotel so our kids can do their laundry tonight, then start on our hunt first thing in the morning. Arlington's only a short drive from Boston, so if we get an early start, we should be able to check in at the mill and then come back and cover several stops on the Freedom Trail as well. Why don't we meet again for dinner tomorrow night, and see what progress each family made? How about if we nominate a winning family based on our results, and the 'losing' family can buy dinner?"

"But, Dad," Adam protested before Mr. and Mrs. Dunn could reply. "We might not get through sixteen stops on the trail all in one day, so how could there be a winner?"

"Adam, whoever gets the farthest on the hunt will win," Mr. Arlington said. "You know we have plans to go to Cape Cod tomorrow night—this is all we'll have time for."

"Sorry, Dad. I just got really excited about competition with the Dunns!"

"We're excited, too," Mrs. Dunn replied, giving Adam an understanding look. "But I think your dad has a good plan—let's see where we are tomorrow night at this time and elect a winner. Then you can continue your vacation plans. We're staying on longer here in Boston, but unless the hunt goes extremely well tomorrow, we probably won't try to finish it after you leave anyway. There may not be much—there may not be anything—to go on."

"Speaking of clues," said her husband, "since each family is going separately, we should decide what to do if we are the first ones to find a clue at a site. It wouldn't really be fair to take it and leave when there's so little to go on. How about if we plan to leave a copy or a description of whatever clue we find with that site's staff and let them know another family may be coming along behind us? Then each family will have an equal chance of success."

"Good idea!" said Mrs. Dunn.

"Done!" said Mr. Arlington. "Happy hunting, and we'll see you here tomorrow night at, say, 6:00."

Both families headed to their hotels for the night, hoping to get an early start on the "race" in the morning.

At their hotel, Ashley and Adam did their camp laundry, repacked their clothes, and fell into bed exhausted. When their parents woke them up at 7:00 the next morning, they still felt tired—until they remembered what was on the agenda for the day.

Usually the whole family started off the day with a jog or a bike ride. Mrs. Arlington was a runner and saw to it her family stayed fit with her, and Adam and Ashley both knew they needed to stay in training to do well in school sports. Mr. Arlington had to stay fit to keep up with the rest of them, but this morning he suggested a swim in the hotel pool, so they could exercise quickly and be on their way. After a spirited workout in the pool, the family picked up some fruit and bagels and headed to their SUV.

On the drive to Arlington, Ashley read from a travel brochure about Arlington's history:

"Arlington, population 44,600. The most significant event in its history took place on April 19, 1775, when British troops met Minutemen gathered from at least thirteen colonial towns there in several skirmishes. At day's end 40 British men were dead and another 80 wounded, while the Americans lost 25 men, with 10 wounded and 3 captured. The town's first industry was cotton manufacturing. In the 1830s an Arlington company began cutting ice from Spy Pond and selling it to tropical countries, establishing a whole new industry.

"The town became a suburb of Boston at the turn of the twentieth century, when Boston's trolley line reached Arlington's boundaries. The town's 11.2-mile Minutemen Bike Trail, which begins in East Arlington and continues through Lexington and Bedford, is a popular attraction for summer cyclists and winter cross-country skiers alike."

Just as Ashley finished reading, the family pulled up in front of the Old Schwab Mill, located on Mill Lane. They immediately looked for the Dunn family's burgundy van with the Michigan license plate, but they didn't see it.

The Arlingtons went inside the mill, and a friendly young woman named Dawn greeted them.

"We're scavenger hunters," Ashley told her. "Our leadership camp was going to sponsor a hunt involving your mill. Do you know anything about this?"

She pulled out the paper with the first clue on it and handed it to Dawn.

"ARLINGTON . . . Old Schwab Mill . . . there 'wood' be an answer there that rings a bell," Dawn read. She thought a minute, then said, "This mill is a living history museum that exhibits a working collection of antique woodworking machines. I can't think of what that would have to do with your scavenger hunt, but I can take you on a tour."

"No bells, or anything else, carved in wood on the machines, that might be meant for us?" Adam asked her.

"Not that I know of, but we can ask around," Dawn answered.

Adam and Ashley looked disappointed.

Seeing their faces, their mother whispered to their dad, "This could be an abrupt ending to the day's fun for them."

"I'd be sorry about that," he whispered back, "but it might mean we'll be visiting our friends and enjoying seafood on Cape Cod sooner. If we don't come up with something after a few hours today, we can call the Dunns on their cell phone and explain to them that the hunt is over."

His wife smiled. Dawn continued to ask staff along the tour route if they'd heard anything about a scavenger hunt, but no one had. As the Arlingtons thanked her and headed toward the front door, though, a worker named Matt came up brushing wood shavings off his shirt.

"Did you say scavenger hunters?" he asked, taking off his safety goggles.

"Yes!" Ashley exclaimed.

"We had ten or twelve wooden bells come in with some sheets of paper a day or two ago in the mail," he said. "But then we got word that the hunt was off, and there was no return address or anything to send them back to."

"So you still have them?" Ashley asked.

"We don't throw things away around here," Matt explained. "We recycle them."

"Great," Adam groaned. "Those bell clues must be wood shavings by now."

Halfway Done, Halfway Defeated

"Not all of them," Matt said. He reached into his apron and pulled out two small wooden bells.

"Not exactly something we'd sell," Matt said. "But someone obviously put in some work on these things, so I thought I'd save a couple. If you guys want one, it's yours."

"Thanks!" Ashley said, accepting the bell.

"Wait a minute!" Matt said. "There was a note, too. It's here somewhere . . ." He shuffled the papers in front of him, but couldn't find it. Then he turned around and looked in the trash can. "Here it is!" he proclaimed triumphantly. "Look, it says, *'Follow the Trail to Freedom.'*" He handed the paper to Mr. Arlington. "Here, you folks take it. I certainly don't have any need for it. I hope it helps."

Mr. Arlington held the paper with *Trail to Freedom* on it next to the one with the *Walk through Time* on it.

"I believe this time line relates to the Freedom Trail," he said. "It mentions Park Street Church, the USS *Consti-*

tution, the State House—if I recall correctly, all those are on the trail."

"That's for sure," Matt said, "and this note says to follow the trail to freedom. It seems to match."

"But our first clue in the cover letter told us to stop at **A**, then do **B-C**," Ashley said. "What could that mean?"

"Only one thing," Matt replied. "Your best bet would be to go to the trail's Information Center on Boston Common—that has to be your **B-C**. I used to work there too. Boston's rich in history, and that reminds me, there was a piece of parchment paper that came with these things. I kept it because I'm a history buff. You can have it too, but I'd sure like to make a copy of it first if you don't mind. Do you want to hear what it says?"

"Absolutely!" the Arlingtons said.

He retrieved it from his back pocket and read aloud:

"The last of the measures inaugurating Britain's new colonial system sparked the greatest organized resistance. Known as the 'Stamp Act,' it ordered that revenue stamps be affixed to all colonial newspapers, broadsides, pamphlets, licenses, leases, or other legal documents, the revenue (collected by American customs agents) to be used for 'defending, protecting and securing' the colonies. The Stamp Act aroused the hostility of most colonists who did any kind of business. Trade with the mother country fell off sharply in the summer of 1765, as prominent men organized themselves into the 'Sons of Liberty'—secret organizations formed to protest the Stamp Act, often through violent means. From Massachusetts to South Carolina, the act was nullified, and mobs, forcing luckless customs agents to resign their offices, destroyed the hated stamps.

"Spurred by delegate Patrick Henry, the Virginia House of Burgesses declared that Virginians could be taxed only by their own representatives. On June 8, the Massachusetts Assembly invited all the colonies to appoint delegates to the so-called Stamp Act Congress in New York, held in October 1765. Twenty-seven representatives from nine colonies came together, and after much debate, this congress adopted a set of resolutions asserting that 'no taxes ever have been or can be constitutionally imposed on them, but by their respective legislatures,' and that the Stamp Act had a 'manifest tendency to subvert the rights and liberties of the colonists.'"

Everyone looked at each other. It was another good bit of history, but no one understood how or if it fit into their search.

"I don't know what you've got there, and I'm not sure you guys know either," Matt said. "But I hope I helped you in some small way. Let me make a copy of this and the note, then you can be on your way."

"Could we ask you another favor?" Mrs. Arlington inquired. "There is one other family—the Dunns—on the scavenger hunt trail with us. We're quite sure they'll be showing up here looking for the same information. Could you make two copies of these papers and let them have one?"

"Certainly," said Matt. "And they are welcome to this other wooden bell; it's obviously a part of the hunt."

"Great!" said Mr. Arlington. "Thanks again."

The Arlingtons headed for their car.

"There are sixteen stops on the Freedom Trail," Ashley said. "What now?"

"We need to begin at the beginning—the **B-C** in the first letter," Adam reminded her. "But since that's where the

Information Center is for the trail, I wonder where we go from there?"

"The sooner we get there, the sooner we can try to find out, and it's still a few hours till lunchtime. Let's head to Boston Common—for the rest of the trip I am Sherlock Holmes," Mr. Arlington said.

Just as the family pulled out of Old Schwab Mill's parking lot onto the main road, a burgundy van pulled in. The people inside all waved at the Arlingtons' SUV, and Ashley and Adam started to wave back.

"Yes!" Adam cheered. "It's the Dunns, and we're ahead of them! So far, so good—they'll be buying the pizza tonight at this rate."

"It's not going to take them as long to get the mill information as it took us, now that we've filled in the staff," Ashley said. "Matt will be waiting for them. Step on it, Dad!"

The Arlingtons headed to downtown Boston and found Boston Common.

"Check it out," Adam said, pointing to a sign. He read:

"America's oldest public park was used until 1830 as a place to graze sheep and cattle. . . . Boston Common, it is said, is anything but common. Never built upon, since 1630 it has gone from a place to graze cattle and sheep to a place to hang pirates, witches, and heretics to a place for the British Army troops to camp . . ."

"A pretty historical place," Ashley commented. She looked around and said, "Hey, look, there's the Information Center. Let's go inside."

The Arlingtons did, and found a woman wearing a name tag that read Madeline.

"Excuse me, can we ask you a couple of questions?" Adam asked. He, Ashley, and their parents introduced themselves to the woman.

"We're on a scavenger hunt," Ashley said. "We don't have a lot of information. We started out in Arlington. But all we have so far is this wooden bell."

"Has anyone come in here to drop anything off in regard to the hunt?" Adam finished.

"I'm sorry, no, and I'd know if they had," Madeline said. "I remember hearing some talk about a scavenger hunt. Other staff along the trail may or may not know something. But I haven't heard anything else about it."

Ashley handed the wooden bell from the mill to Madeline, who looked at it.

"Hey, did you see this?" Madeline asked, holding it upside down. "On the bottom are the letters *N* and *O*."

"Wow!" Adam said. Madeline handed the bell to Adam.

"Is it 'NO' or 'ON'?" Ashley asked.

"I don't know," Adam answered. "It could be either."

"That has to be a clue," Ashley said. "Do you know anything else that might help us?" she asked Madeline.

"Usually, with a scavenger hunt, you have a long list of things to gather, and then you take them somewhere, right?" Madeline asked.

"Ideally, yes," Mrs. Arlington answered. "But our organizer started to put this hunt together and then had to abandon it."

"Yes, everyone but us and one other family has abandoned it," Adam said. "But we're hoping the person who put this together at least got through the part where he planted the clues, or at least left some more information somewhere. We started in Arlington with nothing, but that did lead us to the wooden bells, then here."

Madeline nodded.

"Well, you certainly get perseverance points," she said. "I wonder if your hunt will have any meaning. Obviously, sometimes these kinds of things are nothing but wild goose chases. However, I've seen others that have led to historic discoveries of various kinds—paintings and even jewels, for example."

Adam and Ashley looked at each other and grinned.

"Jewels!" Adam exclaimed. "That would be incredible, wouldn't it?"

Mr. and Mrs. Arlington sighed.

"Let's not get too excited about something that could be, like Madeline said, nothing more than . . . well, nothing," Mr. Arlington advised.

"Whoa, Dad, what happened to Sherlock Holmes?" Ashley asked.

"Excuse us a minute," Mrs. Arlington said. "Alex, over here a second, please."

While the Arlington parents talked, Madeline chatted with Ashley and Adam some more. She filled them in on the history of Boston Common.

"You know, you kids should learn about Samuel Adams. Here," Madeline said, pointing to a TV screen and pressing the button on a remote. "Watch this, and I'll go chat with your parents."

She hit "PLAY," and a tape showing drawings of Boston from long ago began playing. Then up came a picture of Sam Adams, and the narrator on the tape said:

"During a three-year interval of calm, a relatively small number of radical colonists strove to keep the controversy with Britain alive. They contended that payment of the tax would be an acceptance of Parliament's rule over the colonies. They feared that it might have a devastating effect on all colonial liberties. The radicals' most effective leader was Samuel Adams of Massachusetts, who toiled tirelessly for a single end: independence. From the time he graduated from Harvard College in 1740, Adams was a public servant in some capacity. He was a shrewd politician, with the New England town meeting his theater of action. Adams's goals were to free people from their awe of social and political superiors, make them aware of their own power and importance, and thus arouse them to action. He published articles in newspapers and made speeches in town meetings, instigating resolutions that appealed to the colonists' democratic impulses. In 1772 he induced the Boston town meeting to select a 'Committee of Correspondence' to state the rights and grievances of the colonists. Soon similar committees were set up in virtually all the colonies, and out of them grew a base of effective revolutionary organizations. Still, Adams did not have enough fuel to set a fire."

Adam looked at Ashley.

"Samuel Adams was quite a leader, wasn't he?" Adam asked.

"He sure was," Ashley agreed. "He was one who organized and united people toward a common cause. He wanted to empower them—remember, 'empower' was one of the key words at our leadership camp."

Adam did remember. As the two talked, they saw their parents were looking their way.

Mrs. Arlington motioned toward Ashley and Adam.

"The Freedom Trail has a lot of history," Mrs. Arlington said. "Though we can't commit by any means to seeing this search through to the end, we can try and see as much of the Freedom Trail as possible the rest of the day. Let's get going and find as many clues as we can before we meet the Dunns for dinner."

"Awesome," Ashley said.

"Thanks for your time," Adam said to Madeline, shaking her hand.

"You are more than welcome, young man," Madeline said with a smile.

With what little information they had in tow, the Arlingtons headed for the next stop on the trail. Before they hit the beautiful golden dome of the State House, they saw a statue. Mrs. Arlington read from one of the pamphlets they picked up at the visitors' center.

"The Civil War statue is famous because it honors the first African-American troops who risked their lives and potential enslavement to fight for the liberty of America," she read. "It's located on the Black Heritage Trail, which bisects the Freedom Trail here."

The Arlingtons looked at each other, taking in the sociocultural meaning of the statue.

"That's good; it's nice that someone is acknowledging the contribution and key role African-Americans played in the Civil War," Mr. Arlington said.

At the State House, the Arlingtons learned that it didn't always have the striking golden dome atop it. It was a shingled dome until 1802, when Paul Revere and Sons were commissioned to cover it with copper to prevent water leaks. It was gilded for the first time in 1874 and then again in 1997.

"This is the State House, but there is an 'Old State House' a few more stops down the Freedom Trail," Mrs. Arlington pointed out so that no one would be confused.

After their trip to the State House, which yielded no clues and no sight of the Dunns catching up yet, the Arlingtons headed to the Park Street Church at the corner of Park and Tremont streets. Founded in 1809, the building and its 217-foot steeple were, for many years, the first landmark seen by travelers approaching Boston. For nearly two centuries, Park Street Church has organized its life around the Christian gospel and been a pioneer in human concerns. It was the site of a number of important anti-slavery speeches in the early 1800s.

"No clues here either," Ashley reported to the family after checking with a representative of the church.

The family next went to the Granary Burying Ground. With its massive, Egyptian Revival-style gates facing Tremont Street, it is the final resting place of many eminent Revolutionary patriots.

"Wow," Adam said, reading from an informational sheet. "Guess who's buried here? Samuel Adams, Peter Faneuil, Paul Revere, John Hancock . . ."

"That's quite a list," Mr. Arlington noted.

The Arlingtons learned about how the Granary Burying Ground got its current name from the grain storage building, or granary, which once stood on the site where Park Street Church now stands.

Again the family came away with no clues, and Adam and Ashley were starting to feel discouraged. At the next stop, King's Chapel, the Arlingtons were looking for more information about the scavenger hunt. They found another history lesson instead.

"In 1688, the Royal Governor built King's Chapel on the town burying ground when no one in the city would sell him land to build a non-Puritan church," a guide was telling a group of people. "The first King's Chapel was a tiny church used by the King's men who occupied Bostontown to enforce British law. By 1749, the building was too small for the congregation. America's first architect, Peter Harrison, was hired to design on the same site a church 'that would be equal of any in England.' The new church was completed in 1754. The magnificent interior is considered the finest example of Georgian church architecture in North America."

As the family left King's Chapel and turned right down School Street, they noticed a statue of Benjamin Franklin and an accompanying plaque nearby. The statue was the first portrait statue erected in the United States, and it also marked the spot of the first public school, the Boston Latin School, founded in 1635.

"I wish Benjamin Franklin's wisdom could help us now," Adam groaned. "We're coming up with less than nothing. And it's funny we haven't run into the Dunns yet," he commented. "It couldn't have taken them long at the mill in Arlington, and these stops don't take long either. I thought they'd catch up to us by now."

"They could have gone backward around the trail from the other direction," Ashley guessed. "There was nothing in our clues about which way to follow the trail, once we got to Boston Common. What if they tried starting from the end first, and they already have the hunt figured out?"

"It's not the first family done who wins," her mother reminded her. "It's the family who finds the most clues and is closest to figuring all this out by 6:00 tonight. With the scanty information we've found so far, I doubt the Dunns are progressing any better than we are even if they did start from the other end!"

"I doubt it too," their father agreed. "The contact person probably would have gotten the first stops on the trail done before the last stops, and it's beginning to look like he didn't manage to nail down any clues at all other than the Old Schwab Mill. Let's break here for lunch before going on; I'm starving," he said.

They found a nearby restaurant and ordered lunch.

"Counting Boston Common, we've now been to the first half of the stops on the Freedom Trail, and we haven't had a whiff of luck," Mr. Arlington said as they ate. "We'll go to one more place, and if there's no clue there, I'd like to stop. I think that's more than an honest effort on the part of your mother and me. We have people we'd like to see in Cape Cod. We can call the Dunns on their cell phone and tell them they win by default. I'm up for going to the Old Corner Bookstore Building after lunch to see what we can find. If nothing, we're out. If something, we'll take it from there."

Adam glanced despondently toward his sister.

"But, Dad," he said, "we've learned so much. This has been a walking history lesson, just like Mom said. How can we stop now? You just pointed out that we're already halfway through the Freedom Trail!"

"That's true," Mrs. Arlington said. "But our vacation is more than three-quarters done. We want to get down to Cape Cod to see our friends. You and your sister love the beach, and we all love the seafood. We'll have a great time; you'll see. Listen, I'm not saying there's nothing that's going to help us at the next stop. It's just that we haven't had a lot of luck today, and we're several stops into it. You're right—we've all learned a lot already about the history of this area. But we have to prioritize. Whatever happens at the next stop will dictate how the rest of this hunt goes. So don't sweat it. Just enjoy yourself and, like you pointed out, we'll all continue to soak in the incredible history of Boston."

Ashley pulled Adam close to her and whispered in his ear, "Listen, don't be discouraged. We're headed to the Old Corner Bookstore. I have a good feeling about that place. It contains a ton of history, and I've thought from the first time we heard about the Freedom Trail that it was a special place. So don't get worried—at least not yet. Call it a feeling, but I think we're headed in the right direction."

Adam turned and said quietly to her, "I hope you're right, Sis, because if you're not, we're done, and this search is over. But you've liked bookstores even better than toy stores since you were really little. So maybe you're just excited about finding a good book."

"Maybe," Ashley said with a smile. "Maybe not. We'll find out."

Adam agreed. "I just don't want it to end," Adam added, "because if we don't find whatever is out there at the end of this scavenger hunt—if there is, in fact, something out there—it will stay out there. Maybe forever."

New Answers at "Old Corner"

The Old Corner Bookstore Building looked like, well, an old store on a street corner, at the corner of Boston's School and Washington streets. From a distance the Arlingtons could see four people standing out front, two small with dark hair, two large with bright red hair.

"That has to be the Dunns," Adam told his family. "Hey!" he shouted from across the street.

The burly, red-haired man turned toward the shout, then recognized the Arlingtons and waved them over.

"It's our competition!" he laughed. "You move fast—we didn't think we'd ever catch up with you, although we spied you up ahead on the trail a few times this morning. But after the mill, you've left no clues in your wake. How are you doing, or is that top secret information?"

"You can bet we'd have left you clues if we had found any," Mrs. Arlington sighed. "But so far, there's been nothing at all. I'm afraid that unless the Old Corner Bookstore holds more for us than books, we've decided to let you win by default and head to Cape Cod early."

"I can certainly understand that," Mrs. Dunn said. "We've hustled along all morning, getting tired feet and discouraged brains, but the clues just aren't surfacing. We're enjoying the history of Boston, of course, but I'd almost rather be eating lobster on Cape Cod myself. At any rate, we're going to give the bookstore a try now ourselves—let's all go in together," she said.

Both families headed inside. They were approached by a young man whose name tag read Thomas.

"We're looking for information about this terrific bookstore and . . ." Ashley started to tell Thomas.

"I think I can help you out there," Thomas told them enthusiastically before Ashley could finish. "Historic Boston Incorporated bought this building in 1960 to prevent its demolition and to restore its mid-nineteenth-century appearance. It was originally built in 1718 as an apothecary shop and residence, but from 1832 to 1865 Ticknor and Fields Publishing House was located here. That's how it got its current name. Used to be Charles Dickens, Ralph Waldo Emerson, Henry Wadsworth Longfellow, and Henry David Thoreau all frequented it."

"Wow! I love to read, and I've read or heard about a lot of those authors in school," said Ashley.

"Me, too," said Rachel. "It's amazing to think we're standing right where those famous authors spent so much of their time!"

"That's very interesting," Adam said, "but today we're looking for something else." He knew if his sister got started looking at books or discussing authors with Thomas, Rachel, and their parents, they'd forget all about the scavenger hunt and never get out of Old Corner Bookstore until midnight.

Thomas appeared perplexed. "Something else?" he asked.

"Yes," Adam said. "You see, we started this scavenger hunt in Arlington, where we received this." Adam pulled the wooden bell from his pocket. "The rest of the clues are supposed to be on the Freedom Trail."

"You've got to be kidding me!" Thomas said. "What a coincidence. Hold on a minute—I received a box with several wooden book carvings in it, and each is wrapped in a paper. Let me retrieve them from the back."

Ashley, Adam, Rachel, and Ryan could hardly contain their excitement.

"Maybe . . . finally!" Ashley said.

"Let's not get too hopeful," her dad cautioned.

Thomas returned holding two pieces of paper with rubber bands around them. On the counter he unwrapped them, and the pieces of the now-familiar parchment paper and two wooden statues the same size as the bells trickled onto the counter. They were wooden carvings of a book.

"Can we pick them up?" Adam asked Thomas.

"Certainly," Thomas said. "But these might be just as important."

He held up one of the pieces of paper.

"Check it out," Ashley said. "It's 'Old Ironsides' by Oliver Wendell Holmes, dated 1830." She read loudly enough so her family and the Dunns could hear.

Aye, tear her tattered ensign down!
Long has it waved on high,
And many an eye has danced to see
That banner in the sky;

Beneath it rung the battle shout,
And burst the cannon's roar;
The meteor of the ocean air
Shall sweep the clouds no more! . . .

"It's the next clue!" Adam proclaimed, interrupting Ashley. "And look, there's writing on the other side."

Ashley handed Adam the paper, and he read from it:

"The colonies did not consider themselves represented in Parliament unless they actually elected members to the House of Commons. But their idea conflicted with the English principle of 'virtual representation,' by which each member of Parliament represented the interests of the whole country, even if his electoral base was only a tiny minority of property owners. The rest of the community was seen to be 'represented' on the grounds that they all shared the same interests as the property owners who elected members of Parliament.

"Most British officials held that Parliament was an imperial body representing and exercising the same authority over the colonies as over the homeland. The American leaders argued that it was the king who had agreed to establish colonies beyond the sea and the king who provided them with governments. They insisted that the English Parliament had no more right to pass laws for the colonies than any colonial legislature had the right to pass laws for England.

"The British Parliament was unwilling to accept the colonial contentions. British merchants, however, feeling the effects of the American boycott, threw their weight behind a repeal movement, and in 1766 Parliament yielded, repealing the Stamp Act and modifying the Sugar Act. However, Parliament followed these actions with passage of the Declaratory Act, asserting the authority of Parliament to make laws binding the colonies 'in all cases whatsoever.'"

Ashley shook her head in amazement. "How this history unfolded is just incredible," she said.

Thomas nodded. "Ah, that's what this is for—a scavenger hunt," he said. "Surely it's proving educational for you. You know what? These carvings and papers actually came in the mail, and we thought they were souvenirs because there was no mention that they were part of a search or hunt of any kind. I can't stand throwing things away, so I put them aside."

"Well, we sure are glad you did," Mrs. Arlington said. She explained to Thomas the trail they had been on, and how it had grown so cold that the two families had almost stopped.

"You almost 'abandoned ship,'" Thomas said, drawing an analogy to the poem "Old Ironsides."

Adam held out one of the wooden bells to Thomas, who perused it carefully.

As he did, Ashley looked at one of the book carvings. She tipped it upside down.

"This thing has the letters *I* and *T* on the bottom of it!" she said excitedly.

"But what could 'IT' mean?" Adam wondered.

Ashley held a bell and a book carving side by side.

"It could be 'ITON' or 'NOIT' or something like that," Rachel said, trying to link the two clues together using the letters on the bottom of each.

"What will you all do now?" Thomas inquired. "I wish I could be of more help, but this is the only information I can provide. You are welcome to take these with you."

The Arlingtons and the Dunns thanked Thomas and assured him that they would stay on the trail now that they had uncovered another clue.

"The next stop is the Old South Meeting House," Mr. Arlington said. "We've finally found another clue. Do you want to continue, Adam and Ashley?"

Their eyes gave the answer, since they finally had some fuel to add to their curiosity fire.

"You bet!" they exclaimed. "We can't stop now!"

"Looks like we're back in the hunt," Mr. Arlington said to Mr. and Mrs. Dunn and their kids. "I suppose the seafood on Cape Cod will have to wait a little longer for us. We'll head on down the trail to the next stop. Shall we all go together from here?"

"Actually, we haven't stopped for lunch yet, and I'm famished," Mrs. Dunn answered.

Mr. Dunn rubbed his stomach in agreement. "If you're hungry, you can join us," he said to the Arlingtons. "We've got to take a refueling break before we move on."

"We had lunch just before coming here," Mrs. Arlington explained. "We'll go on down the trail, then, but just like at the mill, we'll leave you copies of any clues we find—if we find any more this afternoon . . ."

"Sounds good," Mr. Dunn said. "But don't solve everything while we eat our late lunch! But then, it's who comes closest to figuring it out, not who gets through first, isn't it? We both have till 6 P.M. no matter what we find. If it's a tie, we'll buy you dinner and you can buy us dinner."

They all laughed at that, then said their good-byes and parted ways. The Arlingtons walked toward the Old South Meeting House, reading about its history on their way:

"Built in 1729, the Old South Meeting House was the largest building in colonial Boston. Before the Revolution, people met in it to challenge British rule. Their outrage boiled over on December 16, 1773, when 5,000 colonists came here to protest the tea tax. Their protest resulted in the Boston Tea Party, which sparked the fuel and lit the flame of the American Revolution. Today, you can visit this site where American history was changed forever."

"This is the place where it all really started," Mrs. Arlington told the kids. "What happened here pretty much started a revolution. Let's go inside."

As they entered, they saw a woman who worked there and introduced themselves.

They explained to "Elaine" that they were on a scavenger hunt and showed their clues to her.

"Oh yes, we did receive some information regarding this," Elaine told them.

Adam and Ashley were eager to hear what that was.

"Can you believe it?" Ashley said. "After zero luck all morning, we find clues at two stops in a row!"

Elaine's next statement, however, dashed some of their excitement on that point.

"I'm afraid we couldn't make sense of the box and its contents," Elaine said, "so I'm rather sure we discarded it."

Adam threw his head back, sad that the suddenly red-hot trail had ended out in the all-too-familiar cold.

"Do you remember what the contents were?" Adam pressed her.

"Well, I didn't have time to look too closely—we were quite busy that morning. I seem to remember a coworker saying something about cute little wood carvings, maybe tea bags or something? I've quite forgotten. But they were each wrapped up in paper. I didn't get a look at them, and Sam, the employee who opened the box, isn't here today."

"Thanks anyway," Ashley said to Elaine. Her parents were proud that she remembered to be courteous even though they hadn't found what they were looking for.

"That might be it, then," Mrs. Arlington said to her family as they headed for the door. "That's one clue missing for sure. Ashley and Adam, you two have certainly been persistent, but it wouldn't make sense to go on without an important piece of the puzzle. What do you think, Alex?" she asked her husband.

Just as he started to speak, Elaine caught up with the family and interrupted him.

"Wait!" she said. "I've just been told that I might have something for you after all!"

Cannons and Teapots

Elaine brought over a box. She opened it, and twelve wooden cannons and a piece of parchment spilled out.

"Here you go—I'm guessing this is what you were looking for," Elaine said with a wide smile.

Ashley turned a cannon upside down to look at its base.

"*U T*—what can that mean?" Ashley asked.

Adam pulled the other two carvings from his pocket and tried to make sense of the letters.

If placed in order as they were found, the letters formed "NOITUT"—which no one could make sense of.

"Let's see," Ashley said, unfolding the parchment. The paper had been wet through its travels. Fortunately, the black ink had not run, though the paper was well worn. "It's about the Townshend Acts," she said. She then read it:

"The year 1767 brought more to stir anew all the elements of discord. Charles Townshend, British chancellor of the exchequer, was called upon to draft a new fiscal program. He wanted to reduce British taxes by the more efficient collection of duties on American trade. He sponsored duties on paper, glass, lead, and tea exported from Britain to the colonies.

"The Townshend Acts were designed to raise money to support colonial governors, judges, customs officers, and the British army in America. In response to them, Philadelphia lawyer John Dickinson argued that Parliament had the right to control imperial commerce but did not have the right to tax the colonies.

"The agitation following the Townshend Acts was less violent than that stirred by the Stamp Act, but it was nevertheless strong. Colonists made do with local products. For example, they dressed in homespun clothing, found substitutes for tea, and used homemade paper."

Adam had a thought he wanted to share. "So this Charles Townshend was sort of a leader," he said, "at least in Britain. But you can't lead people like that—from a distance, just telling them what to do. Maybe if he had come to the colonies and explained the financial situation, a lot of these issues might have been able to be resolved without conflict—and maybe without a revolution."

"Well," Mrs. Arlington said, smiling, "there were a lot of events that led to the Revolution. But you have a good point. Good leaders communicate well with those in their charge, and that communication and shared decision making certainly wasn't part of the equation in Britain's dealings with the colonies. Tell people how things are and how they're going to be—without their input or agreement—and sooner or later, that kettle is going to blow."

"That's how it went with the colonies," Elaine affirmed, "and a lot of that steam was built up right here in this place, until the whole thing blew up into the Revolution. These little cannons are a good symbol of that—it took a lot of fighting and sacrifice before the bells of freedom rang."

She paused as they thought about the colonists' bravery and dedication to the cause of independence, then she said, "Here, take these things with you—and I hope they help you on your hunt. Just keep me posted," she smiled.

"Could you keep the cannons for today, except the one we take, and make a copy of this paper to go with them?" said Ashley. "There is another family doing the scavenger hunt, and we should leave something behind for them."

"What, and let this information fall into 'enemy' hands?" asked Elaine. "If you're competing with more families, don't you want to take these clues with you so it's harder for them to beat you? You *are* the first ones to show up and ask for them."

"It's okay," Mr. Arlington laughed. "Only one other family is participating, and we all agreed before starting that we'd do it this way. You see, originally the hunt was called off because, due to unfortunate circumstances, the organizer felt it might not have been completely set up and ready to go. But our family and the Dunns asked for permission to go ahead with it on our own, and we made it into an informal contest. We knew that the clues might be few and far between—if we found any at all. I think it will take all the brain power from both families to get to the bottom of this, so you won't be 'aiding and abetting the enemy' if you help them out after we leave."

With that settled, the Arlingtons headed to the Old State House, Ashley again reading from a pamphlet as they approached: "The Old State House was the headquarters of the British government in Boston. It was built in 1713 and was the symbol of British authority in the colony. The Boston Massacre took place a stone's throw away in 1770, and from the balcony the Declaration of Independence was read aloud in 1776."

As they arrived at the doorway to the Old State House, a woman came out to meet them.

"The Arlingtons?" she asked.

"Yes," Adam answered.

"Elaine just called me to let me know about you and the Dunns, who are with her right now. I have a clue for you!" she explained, introducing herself as Mary. "This is my last day of work; my husband and I are moving to the West Coast for his job. I was literally ready to head out the door when Elaine called. We also got a mysterious box in the mail we couldn't make heads or tails of, so my bosses said I could take it with me. I figured I'd try to track down its meaning by telephone or online later. But Elaine says you can save me the trouble—it will probably make sense to you. It must be a part of the scavenger hunt you are on."

She opened the box and handed Adam a piece of parchment.

"This has to be something to do with our search," Adam said. "Here, I'll read it."

He unfolded the paper, which was in much better shape than the one they found at their last stop, and read it to his family and Mary:

"In 1773 Britain furnished Samuel Adams and his allies with an incendiary issue. The East India Company, in financial straits, appealed to the British government and was granted a monopoly on all tea exported to the colonies. It was also permitted to supply retailers directly, bypassing colonial wholesalers. After 1770 such a flourishing illegal trade existed that most of the tea consumed in America was imported illegally, duty-free. By selling tea through its agents at a much lower price, the East India Company made smuggling unprofitable and threatened to eliminate the independent colonial merchants. Aroused by the loss of the tea trade and the monopolistic practice involved, colonial traders joined in agitating for independence.

"In ports up and down the Atlantic coast, colonial radicals forced East India Company agents to resign, and new shipments of tea were either returned to England or warehoused. In Boston, however, the company's agents defied the colonists and planned to land their tea. On the night of December 16, 1773, a band of men disguised as Mohawk Indians and led by Samuel Adams boarded three British ships lying at anchor and dumped the tea cargo into Boston Harbor.

"A crisis now confronted Britain. The East India Company had carried out a parliamentary statute, and if the destruction of the tea went unpunished, Parliament would admit to the world that it had no control over the colonies. Official opinion in Britain almost unanimously condemned the Boston Tea Party as an act of vandalism and advocated legal measures to bring the insurgent colonists into line."

Ashley waited for Adam to finish.

"The Boston Tea Party is our clue," she deduced.

Mary took the top off of a shoebox and leaned forward. "And that would explain these," she said. She motioned toward Ashley. "Go ahead and take one if you'd like."

The wooden carvings were of a teapot.

"Well, you can't have a tea party without a teapot," Mrs. Arlington said, eliciting a laugh from the group.

"The bottom of it," Ashley remembered, turning it upside down. "There are two more letters, *I* and *T*."

Adam folded his arms. "Those are the same two letters as on the bottom of the book carving," he said.

"Good point," his mother said. "This could be duplicitous, which could throw us offtrack. What do you think, Ashley and Adam?"

Adam and Ashley held the carvings, two each.

"Let's hold them up in the order we retrieved them," Ashley said.

"N-O-I-T-U-T-I-T," Adam said. "That spells nothing."

"It can't be 'nothing,'" Ashley said, breaking into a smile, "because the letters are all wrong."

Everyone chuckled. The search was yielding clues, but nothing that made any sense to anyone yet. Mr. and Mrs. Arlington thought it would be hard for their children to stay focused. However, since they were working so hard, they weren't about to stop the kids on their search. But it was starting to get late, and the other stops along the Freedom Trail would soon be closing for the day.

They looked at a map of the Freedom Trail with Mary.

"Your next two stops are the Boston Massacre site and Faneuil Hall," Mary said. "I'd think that those two places would be logical places for two really good clues."

Adam and Ashley were again wound up. But their mom pointed out that it was almost time to wind the search down, at least for that day.

"We can get to both places if we hurry," Mrs. Arlington said. "But after that, we're calling it a day. The other places will be closing within the hour, and—not to forget the most important factor—we need to meet the Dunns at the restaurant at 6:00. I wonder how they're coming along?"

Steak—Not Lobster

The Arlingtons next headed to the Boston Massacre site, a ring of cobblestones on what is now a traffic island. Standing outside the ring were Mr. and Mrs. Dunn, Rachel, and Ryan.

"We just thought we'd check out this site on our way into the Old State House," Mr. Dunn told the Arlingtons. "There's some fascinating history here, but no clues. Should we hope for any clues over there?"

"Definitely!" Adam said. "Ask for Mary; she'll be expecting you."

"But don't take long," Mrs. Arlington added. "She was about to leave work—for good."

The Dunns said good-bye and quickly headed over to find Mary.

The Arlington kids knew that their parents' goal was to make the scavenger hunt, first and foremost, a learning experience, so Ashley took the time to read to her family the details of the site that were posted, even though they knew there were no clues to be found there:

"In Boston, enforcement of the new regulations provoked violence. British customs officials collecting duties were sometimes roughly handled by the colonists, so two British regiments were dispatched to protect them. The presence of British troops in Boston invited disorder. On March 5, 1770, what began as a harmless snowballing of British soldiers degenerated into a mob attack. Someone gave the order to fire. When the smoke cleared, five men lay dead, three of them Bostonians. Among them was Crispus Attucks, the first black man to die in the Revolution."

The family picked up some flyers nearby and some bottled water and sat down on a bench to rest. One flyer looked particularly intriguing. It contained the text of John Hancock's "Boston Massacre Oration," which he gave in Boston in 1774, four years after the massacre.

"This is pretty long, but it's powerful stuff," Adam said. "We can read the whole thing later, but how about if I just read some of the final paragraph for now?" He read aloud:

"I have the most animating confidence that the present noble struggle for liberty will terminate gloriously for America. And let us play the man for our God, and for the cities of our God; while we are using the means in our power, let us humbly commit our righteous cause to the great Lord of the Universe, who loveth righteousness and hateth iniquity. And . . . let us joyfully leave our concerns in the hands of him who raiseth up and pulleth down the empires and the kingdoms of the world as he pleases . . ."

After resting a little and finishing their water and the final paragraph of Hancock's famous speech, the family headed to Faneuil Hall. Dubbed the "Cradle of Liberty," Faneuil Hall was the site of many fiery town meetings after it was built in 1742 by Boston merchant Peter Faneuil and given as a gift to the town.

The Arlingtons hoped the hall would give them the gift of one more clue for the day, but it was not to be. The Faneuil Hall staff were pleasant and had lots of historical information to offer, but no clues at all to help with the scavenger hunt. Still, the family picked up some more fact booklets full of information about the events leading up to the Revolution. As they looked them over, the Dunns walked in the door.

"Everything's about to close down for the day," Ryan said as his family greeted the Arlingtons. "This was going to be our last stop for the day. Is this as far as you got too?"

"It sure is," said Mr. Arlington. "We were about to read some of the history from these booklets, then drive over to the restaurant for our 6:00 appointment with you. You won't find any more clues here, but the historical facts the staff provided are interesting enough. Do you want to look them over together, then head out for dinner?"

"Sounds great," Mr. Dunn agreed. "What do you have there? It's about time I took a turn to read, since my wife and daughter have been doing most of it today."

Mrs. Arlington handed him the booklet she had been about to read from, and he started off in a booming voice that attracted several more tourists, who joined the families' group to listen:

"Parliament responded to the Boston Tea Party with new laws that the colonists called the 'Five Intolerable Acts.' The first, the Boston Port Bill, closed the port of Boston until the ruined tea was paid for—an action that threatened the very life of the city. To prevent Boston from having access to the sea meant economic disaster. Some of the other enactments restricted local authority and banned town meetings held without the governor's consent.

"Instead of subduing Massachusetts as Parliament intended, these acts rallied its sister colonies to come to its aid. At the suggestion of the Virginia House of Burgesses, colonial representatives met in Philadelphia on September 5, 1774, 'to consult upon the present unhappy state of the Colonies.' This meeting became known as the First Continental Congress. Every colony except Georgia sent at least one delegate, the total number reaching fifty-five.

"The Congress resolved that no obedience was due the Intolerable Acts and maintained the right of the colonists to 'life, liberty and property.' It also maintained that colonial legislatures held the right to set all cases of taxation. Most importantly, it formed a Continental Association that soon assumed leadership in the colonies. Under the association, new local groups began to collect military supplies, mobilize troops, and fan public opinion into revolutionary ardor.

"The colonies were divided in their opinions toward the British Crown, which presented a genuine dilemma for the delegates. They needed to appear unanimous in their opposition if they were to induce Britain to make concessions to the colonies. At the same time, however, they would have to avoid showing any radicalism that would alarm more moderate Americans, many of whom felt that discussion and compromise with the Crown was the proper solution. The king could have made allies of these moderates and, by granting concessions, strengthened them and made it more difficult for the revolutionaries to proceed. But George III had no intention of making concessions. In late 1774 he wrote, 'The die is now cast, the Colonies must either submit or triumph.'"

"Those were fighting words!" Adam exclaimed.

"They sure were!" agreed Ryan.

"Yes, and many colonists, some of them young like you, lived in danger and even sacrificed their lives to earn that triumph," said Mrs. Arlington. It was a sobering thought for them all.

"Let's go to the next stop, Paul Revere's House. He's my favorite patriot," said Ryan. "I would have liked to be with him on his midnight ride—dangerous or not, it had to be one of the most exciting moments of his life!"

"I'm sure it was, son, but visiting Revere House will have to wait until tomorrow. It's closing time for the Freedom Trail, and time for us to go have dinner," Mrs. Dunn said.

Her husband and Mr. and Mrs. Arlington agreed.

"Do we want pizza again, or should we add some variety?" Mr. Arlington said. "We were supposed to meet at the pizza place, but since we're all together, we could go anywhere."

"I have a taste for a big steak," said the burly Mr. Dunn, "but that's a little more expensive than pizza, and we haven't decided who has 'won' the scavenger hunt and who is buying tonight. Even though we all ended up with the same clues, you Arlingtons have been ahead of us on the trail most of the day, so I guess I'm volunteering . . ."

"Could my wife and I have just a minute to discuss it?" Mr. Arlington asked. "Ashley and Adam, wait here with the Dunns; I need to speak to your mother."

Mr. and Mrs. Arlington stepped aside to have a private conference, and when they came back, they were smiling ear to ear.

"Let's go enjoy a steak dinner together and split the cost, but let's not pick a winning family just yet," Mr. Arlington said. "Anne and I have decided that it makes sense for us to stay on at least part of one more day and see this thing through with Ashley and Adam, and with you. Kids, we're so proud of the way you've stuck with this hunt and the way you've taken an interest in learning the history of Boston even when you were disappointed at not finding more clues. With Paul Revere's House, *Old Ironsides,* and other fascinating stops still ahead, how can we stop now? The lobsters on Cape Cod will still be there if we're a little late."

It was Adam and Ashley's turn to smile ear to ear, and Rachel and Ryan joined them. The Arlington teens knew they were cutting deeply into the time their parents had planned to spend on Cape Cod eating seafood and visiting their friends.

"All right! You and Mom have been great about this," Adam told his dad. "You don't have to do this for us, though. If we have to hang it up now, I can live with it."

No Time to Quit

Ashley was stunned that her brother was ready to give in. She looked at him like he was an alien from outer space.

"What? Wave the white flag now?" she whispered in his ear. "We need another day—that's all!"

Adam whispered back, "But you have to admit, it's getting frustrating not finding many clues, and Mom and Dad have been really patient . . ."

Ashley had to agree. After thinking a minute, she finally said, "He's right, Mom and Dad. I'm having a really good time doing the scavenger hunt, especially with Rachel, Ryan, and Mr. and Mrs. Dunn involved."

She looked toward the Dunn family and smiled. They were standing by quietly while the Arlingtons worked out what they wanted to do.

"I can live with it too, though, if you want to quit now and drive to Cape Cod for lobster dinner," she finished, forcing herself to smile at her parents.

"We appreciate that, kids, but now is no time to quit!" said Mr. Arlington. "Your mom and I have made up our minds, and I'll still get lobster dinner—just a day later."

"We couldn't give up now," Mrs. Arlington added. "As King George III said, the die is now cast, we must either submit or triumph. I don't know if we can triumph, given the scarcity of clues and information, but we've found out some interesting things today—we're not ready to submit! All four of you kids have pursued this thing vigorously. You've found answers when it appeared none were in sight, and you've kept up a winning attitude even when you couldn't find them. We're proud of you. So let's hit this hunt hard again tomorrow, and then we'll go from there."

"Terrific! I'm so glad you're all still in the game," Mr. Dunn interrupted. "But can we go from *here* now? I'll be the one quitting—from starvation—if we don't get some dinner in the next half hour!"

The families shared a hearty laugh, and after agreeing on the restaurant, they found their cars and their appetites.

After a huge steak dinner with the Dunns, the Arlingtons drove back to their hotel exhausted. Mr. and Mrs. Arlington decided to wind down in the hotel's hot tub before bed. Back in their room, Adam hooked up his laptop computer to go online, planning to research some of the information along the next day's Freedom Trail stops. He put his head back on his pillow for a minute, though, and fell fast asleep, with his computer blinking next to him on the bed.

Ashley noticed and put down the day's pamphlets she had been reading. Adam was usually the computer expert who did the research, gathered the information, and even planned the routes for their vacation trips using the Internet. He was out cold, though, and his laptop was all hooked up, ready to surf the web.

Ashley gently lifted his computer off his bed, and trailing wires, placed it on hers. Sitting down in a chair next to her bed, she went to the Freedom Trail's web site, www.thefreedomtrail.org, and read more about the history along the path. While the sites along the trail went in geographical order, they didn't necessarily go in chronological order, so she pieced together the parchment papers they had collected and worked to develop a picture of the history they had learned in her mind.

Her mother and father came back from relaxing in the hot tub, entering quietly when they saw Adam was already sound asleep.

"Don't stay up too late," Mrs. Arlington whispered to Ashley, brushing back her daughter's hair with her hand. "We could have a long day tomorrow."

"Okay, I'll log off soon," Ashley said. "I wasn't even going to do this, but Adam logged on and fell right asleep."

Mr. and Mrs. Arlington laughed at that.

"It isn't often he prefers sleep to being on the computer," Mr. Arlington said. "But right now your mother and I do prefer sleep, so we're off to bed." He kissed his daughter good night while Mrs. Arlington covered Adam, who stirred but didn't awaken.

After her parents turned in for the night, Ashley decided to search online for information about a revolutionary hero they hadn't learned much about on the trail yet, but whom she had been studying in school—Patrick Henry.

"As a revolutionary patriot, statesman, and orator, Patrick Henry expressed the colonists' growing unhappiness with imperial rule in his Stamp Act speech of 1765 and his famous Liberty or Death speech of 1775," she read. "He served five one-year terms as governor of Virginia, and he opposed Virginia's ratification of the Constitution of the United States in 1788 because the document originally contained no Bill of Rights. After its ratification, he worked to assure that its first ten amendments were added."

Ashley found his famous Liberty or Death speech, which he gave on March 23, 1775. Part of it stated:

"The questing before the House is one of awful moment to this country. For my own part, I consider it as nothing less than a question of freedom or slavery; and in proportion to the magnitude of the subject ought to be the freedom of the debate. . . . Should I keep back my opinions at such a time, through fear of giving offense, I should consider myself as guilty of treason towards my country, and of an act of disloyalty toward the Majesty of Heaven, which I revere above all earthly kings."

She read through the rest and jotted down these words, which gave her a lump in her throat as she read them:

". . . They tell us, sir, that we are weak; unable to cope with so formidable an adversary. But when shall we be stronger? Will it be the next week, or the next year? Will it be when we are totally disarmed, and when a British guard shall be stationed in every house? . . . We shall not fight our battles alone. There is a just God who presides over the destinies of nations, and who will raise up friends to fight our battles for us. The battle, sir, is not to the strong alone; it is to the vigilant, the active, the brave . . ."

The speech was longer than Ashley had known, but each sentence was well crafted and held deep meaning. Ashley slowed down to read the ending carefully, since it was where the most famous words of the speech were:

"Gentlemen may cry, 'Peace, Peace'—but there is no peace. The war is actually begun! The next gale that sweeps from the north will bring to our ears the clash of resounding arms! Our brethren are already in the field! Why stand we here idle? What is it that gentlemen wish? What would they have? Is life so dear, or peace so sweet, as to be purchased at the price of chains and slavery? Forbid it, Almighty God! I know not what course others may take; but as for me, give me liberty or give me death!"

Ashley realized that Patrick Henry was a great leader. He was obviously among the most articulate men of his time. His points were both well thought out and well made.

"He didn't just say what people wanted to hear," Ashley thought to herself. "He told them the truth, giving them a short-term vision and a long-term resolution, and the sacrifice that was necessary for freedom. And then when freedom was achieved, he went out on a limb to make sure everyone's individual freedom was addressed by pursuing the Bill of Rights, even when it would have been easier to just go along and ratify the Constitution without it. But he stuck to his principles, which all good leaders do no matter the consequences."

Then Ashley read about Paul Revere's House, which was the next stop the family planned to make on the Freedom Trail the following morning. The text described Paul Revere's exciting ride and courageous life:

"In 1774 and the spring of 1775 Paul Revere was employed by the Boston Committee of Correspondence and the Massachusetts Committee of Safety as an express rider to carry news, messages, and copies of resolutions as far away as New York and Philadelphia. On the evening of April 18, 1775, Paul Revere was sent for by Dr. Joseph Warren and instructed to ride to Lexington, Massachusetts, to warn Samuel Adams and John Hancock that British troops were marching to arrest them.

"After being rowed across the Charles River to Charlestown, Paul Revere borrowed a horse from his friend Deacon John Larkin and verified that the local 'Sons of Liberty' had seen his prearranged signals—two lanterns had been hung briefly in the bell tower of Christ Church in Boston, indicating that British troops would row 'by sea' across the Charles River to Cambridge, rather than marching 'by land' out Boston Neck. (Revere had arranged for these signals the previous weekend, as he was afraid that he might be prevented from leaving Boston.)

"On the way to Lexington, Revere 'alarmed' the countryside, stopping at each house. He arrived in Lexington about midnight. As he approached the house where Adams and Hancock were staying, a sentry asked that he not make so much noise.

"'Noise!' cried Revere, 'you'll have noise enough before long. The Regulars are coming out!'

"After delivering his message, Revere was joined by a second rider, William Dawes, who had been sent on the same errand by a different route. Deciding on their own to continue on to Concord, Massachusetts, where weapons and supplies were hidden, Revere and Dawes were joined by a third rider, Dr. Samuel Prescott. Soon after, all three were arrested by a British patrol. Prescott escaped almost immediately, and Dawes soon after. Revere was held for some time and then released. Left without a horse, Revere returned to Lexington in time to witness part of the battle on the Lexington Green."

Ashley folded her arms across her body and leaned back in the chair, wondering what it was like in the late 1700s in Boston.

"Miss Ashley, Miss Ashley!" a voice called out from the porch next door.

"Yes?" Ashley answered, "What is it?"

"Paul Revere just rode by, and the British are coming!" the woman said. "He stopped next door and told Hancock and Adams that the British are on their way!"

Ashley stood still in amazement. Certainly it was a shock to no one that it had come to this, especially after the events that had transpired in the past weeks, months, and even years. Still, to have the hour finally here was overwhelming in many ways.

"Patrick Henry was right in his speech one month ago to this exact day," Ashley said to the woman. "Indeed, it will be liberty or death, because the fruits of liberty provide sustenance, while oppression will eventually wear out the life in our very souls."

Dust was flying, illuminated by the midnight moon. Though most households had been asleep for several hours, lanterns could be seen in windows as colonists dressed and men grabbed their weapons. Chaos was all around. The hope for independence for the colonies was reaching a critical stage.

The cold air didn't faze Ashley as she stepped outside, closing the door to the house behind her. She had a rifle in her hand and equal parts courage and fear in her heart. The fight for independence would, indeed, be a fight. The war of words was over. The real fight for freedom, Ashley realized, lay ahead—right in the road passing in front of her house.

"This is the cost for independence," Ashley said to the woman who had joined her. "The price will be high. As Patrick Henry says, it's 'liberty or death.' No one should have to live under rules set by others when no voice of their own is included in the decision making."

Ashley felt a hand on her shoulder.

"No price too high!" Ashley said.

"For what?" a voice answered.

Ashley opened her eyes, and it was her father trying to wake her.

"You fell asleep, Ash," he said. He added with a grin, "You were talking about high prices, and it didn't sound like it had anything to do with shopping."

"Oh yes, right, Dad," Ashley said. "I was just looking up some stuff online about Patrick Henry and Paul Revere."

Ashley looked at the clock. It was past 10:30 P.M., and she knew that the family would probably awaken around 7 or 8 A.M.

"I'm off to bed," Ashley said. Her father headed back to his bedroom, and Ashley decided to call it a night. She logged off Adam's laptop, turned out the light, and fell fast asleep herself, wondering if she would dream again of Boston and the Revolution.

A Clue Ships Out

The following morning, the Arlingtons got up and headed down to the hotel's pool and workout area. Adam and Mrs. Arlington swam while Ashley and her father ran on treadmills.

After a light breakfast, the family headed to Paul Revere's House, which was the next stop on the Freedom Trail. Ashley was already well versed in the man whose midnight ride went down in history as leading the country even farther down the road toward independence.

On their tour the Arlingtons heard about the famous ride, and how Revere expanded his business interests in the years following the Revolution.

"He imported goods from England and ran a small hardware store until 1789," said a guide at the house. "By 1788 he had opened a foundry that supplied bolts, spikes, and nails for North End shipyards, including brass fittings for the USS *Constitution*. The foundry also produced cannons and, after 1792, cast bells. One of his largest bells still rings in Boston's King's Chapel.

"Since Revere was concerned that the United States had to import sheet copper from England, he opened the first copper rolling mill in North America in 1801. He provided copper sheeting for the hull of the USS *Constitution* and for the dome of the new Massachusetts State House in 1803. Revere Copper and Brass, Inc., the descendant of Revere's rolling mill, is best known for Revereware copper-bottomed pots and pans. (Revereware is now, however, manufactured by another company.)

"Revere's community and social involvements were extensive. The son of an immigrant artisan, not born to wealth or inheritance, Revere became a modestly well-to-do businessman and a popular local figure of some note.

"Revere died of natural causes on May 10, 1818, at the age of eighty-three, leaving five children and several grandchildren and great-grandchildren. An obituary in the *Boston Intelligence* commented, 'seldom has the tomb closed upon a life so honorable and useful.' Paul Revere is buried in Boston's Granary Burying Ground."

The Arlingtons' guide, Alvin, could provide no clues to the Arlingtons' scavenger hunt search, even after checking with the other workers.

"I guess Ted ran into another family earlier this morning asking the same questions you're asking me," Alvin told the Arlingtons. "He had to tell them what I'm telling you—apparently no clues were left here with us for you. Better luck at your next stop!"

The family thanked him for being such a knowledgeable guide and moved down the trail.

"I guess Rachel and her family got the jump on us this morning," Ashley commented as they headed toward the Old North Church. "Do you think we'll catch up with them?"

"That depends on what they find, I suppose. They're the ones breaking ground for us today, and it takes longer to uncover a clue than just to visit a site and absorb the history," said her father.

The Arlingtons discovered that the Old North Church, built in 1723, is the oldest church building in Boston. On April 8, 1775, the church's sexton, Robert Newman, set out two lanterns to warn Paul Revere and others of British troop movements. Episcopal church services are still held there today, but the church held no clue for the Dunns or Arlingtons.

After that, the Arlingtons visited Copp's Hill Burying Ground, the final resting place of merchants, artisans, and craftspeople who lived and worked in the North End. Also buried there are thousands of free blacks who lived during colonial times in the nearby "New Guinea Community." Because of its height, the British used this vantage point to train their cannons on Charlestown during the Battle of Bunker Hill.

Again, though, the site held no clues to the scavenger hunt.

"There are just two stops left," Mr. Arlington said to Adam and Ashley. "Those stops might yield something—or they might yield nothing at all. Regardless, we'll head to the USS *Constitution* and then to Bunker Hill and see if anything turns up."

That was good enough for Adam and Ashley.

The USS *Constitution,* the second to the last stop, is still part of the U.S. Navy and is staffed as a regular military assignment by active-duty sailors.

The Arlingtons talked to the men and women working on board the ship. They had little luck finding a scavenger hunt clue, but did listen intently as they learned about *Old Ironsides.*

"Nicknamed *Old Ironsides,* the USS *Constitution* is the oldest commissioned ship in the United States Navy. Construction began in November of 1794, and the ship didn't have a successful launch into the water until the third try, on September 23, 1797," said Petty Officer Kathy Kuhl. "The ship is said to weigh nearly 1,600 tons. It had on board at one time up to 400 men and a complement of 44 guns. The ship was built at a cost to the U.S.'s young Navy of $302,719, a huge financial commitment at the time. Although she never lost a battle, her most famous engagement was with the HMS *Guerriere* in the War of 1812. After an extended battle, the captain of the *Constitution* asked if the *Guerriere* wished to surrender or 'Strike her flag.' The response from the French Captain Dacres was, 'Well, I don't know; our mainmast is gone; our mizzenmast is gone, and upon the whole you may say that we *have* struck our flag.' The *Constitution* received nothing but superficial scars to her copper-clad hull, earning her the famous nickname *Old Ironsides.*

"In 1830 the Navy decided to break up the old ship, rotting in her berth in Charlestown. Upon hearing of the decision, a Cambridge law student, Oliver Wendell Holmes, wrote the poem 'Old Ironsides,' which so stirred the public that the Navy changed its decision. Since then the ship has been refurbished and now stands as one of America's most treasured artifacts."

As Kuhl finished her talk, Ryan approached her. Around her shoulder he saw someone with a head of red hair approaching from the other side.

"Ryan?" he asked.

"You finally caught up with us!" Ryan said to him with a grin. "We were listening to Petty Officer Kuhl's talk from over on the other side."

Kuhl smiled at the boys and asked, "Did you enjoy seeing the ship?"

"It's awesome!" said Adam, "but can we ask you something?"

"Absolutely," she replied. "That's what I'm here for."

Adam pulled out their copy of the parchment with Oliver Wendell Holmes's famous poem "Old Ironsides" on it. Ryan showed her that he had one too.

"Have you seen this before?" Adam asked.

"I've seen something like this," Kuhl said. "What's it all about?"

Adam almost jumped out of his shoes at her answer. He quickly explained the two families' scavenger hunting thus far. The rest of the Arlingtons and Dunns had gathered around her by this time and helped fill in the details of his story.

"Let me check on this, because one of our other sailors, Andy Toler, had them," Kuhl said. "I was on weekend leave, so I haven't been around the past few days."

She went and checked with another sailor who was located just off the ship. Anticipating a new and special clue, no one in the group was prepared for Kuhl's next words.

"Well, I have some good news and I have some bad news," Kuhl said. "We did receive a box that had something like what you described in it. The bad news is we couldn't make heads or tails out of it. So Andy either disposed of the box or took it with him."

Adam looked at his father.

"Perhaps we could call this man?" Mr. Arlington asked.

"That would be the bad news part: Toler shipped out Saturday morning," Kuhl said. "He was going to visit his family in New York, and then he was heading to Australia either this afternoon or tomorrow."

"Oh no!" Ashley said.

Mrs. Arlington grabbed her daughter's hand. "Is there any way whatsoever of contacting him?" she asked.

Kuhl thought about that for a moment.

"I think I have his e-mail address in my notebook," she said. "I could probably get a message to him. But I don't know how many days—or even weeks—it might take for him to receive the message. He might not have access to his e-mail until he arrives at his station. It's a long trip to Australia."

The Arlingtons knew that to be true. The plane trip they took to watch the 2000 Olympic Games in Sydney took almost twenty-two hours.

"We can try to reach him in a day or two when he gets there," Mr. Arlington said.

Kuhl looked down. She didn't want to tell the Arlingtons and Dunns what she knew, but she felt she had to.

"Sir," Kuhl said to Mr. Arlington, "he's going on assignment by Navy boat. I don't think he'll be there for months."

One-of-a-Kind Clue

The Arlingtons and Dunns thanked Petty Officer Kuhl for her help. As they got off the ship, Mr. Arlington stopped and turned around.

"I'll be right back," he told everyone.

He went up to Kuhl and pulled out a business card. On the back of it he scribbled down their hotel number.

"If anything comes up, or if someone else coming in on a later shift knows anything, please feel free to contact us," he told her. "We'd really appreciate it."

Kuhl said she'd check with the next crew, which was due in within the hour.

As the two families walked down the pier, they were despondent over this latest development. They decided to part ways temporarily, since the Arlingtons weren't heading to the next stop on the Freedom Trail until after lunch.

Mr. and Mrs. Arlington had to return to the hotel first to take care of some business.

When they arrived at the hotel, Mr. Arlington checked to see if a fax had arrived that he was expecting from his office in Washington, D.C. The man at the desk instead handed him a box.

Adam, Ashley, and their mother were standing across the lobby, trying to decide what they would do for lunch. No one was really hungry, though. Their appetites had been stunted by the development earlier at *Old Ironsides*.

But as their father approached, Adam and Ashley saw what he was carrying.

"This was dropped off about fifteen minutes ago by Petty Officer Kuhl," Mr. Arlington said.

Adam wanted to open the box right away.

"Let's head up to the room," his dad said. "That way we can go through it."

Adam tucked the box under his arm, and the family headed toward the middle lobby. The elevator seemed to take forever, and Adam and Ashley didn't want to wait.

"Okay if we take the stairs?" Adam asked.

Mrs. Arlington rolled her eyes. "That's fifteen floors," she said. "But if you want to . . ."

"We need the exercise," Ashley said with a grin. She and Adam headed to the stairs, taking two at a time. Sure enough, by the time they got to the fifteenth floor, their parents were already at the door to their room. Ashley and Adam were out of breath, but hardly daunted.

They opened the box on the table in the living room of the suite. Several wooden carvings of a boat tumbled out.

"We already have this one," Adam said dejectedly.

Ashley picked one up and turned it over. "New letters!" she said. "There is an *SN* on the bottom of it."

Adam pulled the other carvings out of his backpack.

"Now we have 'N-O-I-T-U-T-I-T-S-N'—although it still makes no sense," Adam said.

Everyone else examined the letters. Ashley pulled out the piece of parchment paper that had been wrapped around the carving. She read it:

"In January, 1776, Thomas Paine, a political theorist and writer who had come to America from England in 1774, published a fifty-page pamphlet, *Common Sense*. Within three months, 100,000 copies of the pamphlet were sold. Paine attacked the idea of hereditary monarchy, declaring that one honest man was worth more to society than 'all the crowned ruffians that ever lived.' He presented the alternatives—continued submission to a tyrannical king and an outworn government, or liberty and happiness as a self-sufficient, independent republic.

"Circulated throughout the colonies, *Common Sense* helped to crystallize the desire for separation. There still remained the task, however, of gaining each colony's approval of a formal declaration. On May 10, 1776—one year to the day since the Second Continental Congress had first met—a resolution was adopted calling for separation. On June 7, Richard Henry Lee of Virginia introduced a resolution declaring 'That these United Colonies are, and of right ought to be, free and independent states. . . .' Immediately, a committee of five, headed by Thomas Jefferson of Virginia, was appointed to prepare a formal declaration."

Ashley handed it to Adam to finish reading.

"Largely Jefferson's work, the Declaration of Independence, adopted July 4, 1776, not only announced the birth of a new nation, but also set forth a philosophy of human freedom that would become a dynamic force throughout the entire world," Adam read. "The Declaration draws upon French and English Enlightenment political philosophy, but one influence in particular stands out: John Locke's *Second Treatise on Government.* Locke took conceptions of the traditional rights of Englishmen and universalized them into the natural rights of all humankind. The Declaration's familiar opening passage echoes Locke's social-contract theory of government:

> We hold these truths to be self-evident, that all men are created equal, that they are endowed by their Creator with certain unalienable Rights, that among these are Life, Liberty and the pursuit of Happiness. That to secure these rights, Governments are instituted among Men, deriving their just powers from the consent of the governed, that whenever any Form of Government becomes destructive of these ends, it is the Right of the People to alter or to abolish it, and to institute a new Government, laying its foundation on such principles, and organizing its powers in such form, as to them shall seem most likely to effect their Safety and Happiness.

"In the Declaration, Jefferson linked Locke's principles directly to the situation in the colonies. To fight for American independence was to fight for a government based on popular consent in place of a government by a king. Only a government based on popular consent could secure natural rights to life, liberty, and the pursuit of happiness."

The family went through the rest of the wooden ship carvings, all replicas of the one they were looking at. Mr.

and Mrs. Arlington retreated to their bedroom so he could change into more comfortable shoes and she could grab a sweater.

"Do you think all the parchment papers have the same message?" Ashley wondered aloud.

"Sure," Adam said, "why not? That's the way it was with all the other clues."

Adam and Ashley unrolled each of the papers anyway. A small piece of white paper fell out of one.

"Bingo!" Ashley said. "Look at this!"

Her parents heard Ashley's call and quickly came out.

"What is it, Ash?" her dad asked.

She unfolded the white paper.

"Only the person who gets this particular carving will win the scavenger hunt," the note read. "Hopefully everyone else learned a magnificent history lesson. But only the recipient of this paper will be able to solve the mystery. Because things aren't as they a pier, and the water does hold the answer. Take the plunge. Your last clue spells out exactly where to find the answer. You will return to the meeting place for your final clue. And then you can finish your scavenger hunt and find your reward."

The Arlingtons looked at each other in astonishment.

"So if we hadn't received the exact carving that had the parchment paper with the white sheet of paper tucked inside, we would have been out of luck?" Adam asked.

"It looks like it," his mom answered. "It must be a one-of-a-kind clue. Count this as a blessing—that we were able to procure the whole box of these things. Who knows if we missed anything else at the other stops, since we took just one carving and one written clue at each place."

Adam agreed. "And Dad—I mean, Sherlock Holmes—gets credit for the 'save' of the trip," he said.

"How's that?" his dad asked.

"Remember," Adam said, "you decided to go back to Petty Officer Kuhl and give her the hotel number and your business card. If you hadn't done that, we wouldn't have gotten this, our most important clue so far."

Mrs. Arlington patted her husband on the back. "That's right, and none of us thought of it, so you saved the day," she said to him. "Good work, Sherlock."

"Sherlock" was glad he had had a role in helping advance the hunt, especially since it meant so much to the kids. However, he had a question.

"What about the Dunns?" he asked his family.

"Oh wow, this puts us ahead of them—this means we win!" Adam shouted.

"Not so fast," his father said. "We agreed to leave clues for each other all along the way, but this time we got the whole box. They didn't even have a chance at this one."

"Well, that's not really true, Dad," Ashley pointed out. "You were the one who thought about going back to give Petty Officer Kuhl your business card in case any new information turned up. The rest of us, including the Dunns, were on our way off the *Constitution.*"

"So you're saying I should be declared the winner by myself?" Mr. Arlington asked.

"Not exactly," said Ashley. "After all, you are on *our* team, so we should get the credit too. But I think that to be completely fair to Rachel and Ryan and their mom and dad, we would have to wrap all these carvings back up in the parchment papers, with one of them having the white paper hidden in it. Then each family could pick one—after all, that's how it would have happened if we got one at the ship like was planned for this hunt. But now, this way, if either family gets the white paper, they would win. If no one gets it, we would tie."

"She's right," Adam said. "This hunt is not happening 'normally' like it was supposed to, so it's not really fair that we ended up with this whole box of carvings, even though it was 'Sherlock Dad's' quick thinking that got it for us."

"I'm really proud of the two of you," Mrs. Arlington commented to her kids. "You are absolutely right that this hunt is not going 'normally' as planned, and that these are unusual circumstances. And we could have easily claimed this special clue and declared ourselves the winners with it. But we've always taught you that it's more important to be fair than to win, and I can see that you've taken that to heart. I'm so glad!

"I have an idea. Why don't we call the Dunns on their cell phone and let them in on what we have here? We can meet them at the final stop, Bunker Hill, and work on solving the rest of the mystery—if that's possible—together. I think we'd all agree that declaring a winning family isn't that important anymore. We are just so close to solving what looked like an impossible thing—it may take all eight of us together to finish pulling it off. What do you think?"

"Under these circumstances, I think that's entirely true," said Mr. Arlington. "What about you two—will you be disappointed if we're not the 'winning' family because of sharing this with the Dunns?"

"No way! No problem!" said Adam.

Ashley agreed. "I'm going to be so excited if we actually discover the reward at the end of this thing that I'll be perfectly happy to have two winning families—working together," she said.

The family decided to get lunch and then head to Bunker Hill to meet the Dunns. They called to let the Dunns in on the new clues and set a meeting time. As they talked over lunch, Mr. and Mrs. Arlington wanted to make sure the kids had the right perspective entering what could be the final phase of the hunt.

"You two have done a very good job getting this far," Mrs. Arlington said. "But your father and I want you to be aware that this could still just be a wild goose chase. The end of this rainbow might not hold any pot of gold. We just don't want you to be let down. To get this far, you have shown great tenacity and commitment to see this thing through. But to see it through to what? We just don't know. We could find something—we could find nothing. Just don't get your hopes up too high. The 'reward' could be nothing more than a certificate, or it could be something else. We simply don't know at this point, all right?"

Ashley and Adam assured their parents that they understood completely. Then the Arlingtons took off for Bunker Hill, the final stop on the Freedom Trail. They had already been there for the informational meeting about the scavenger hunt, so they wondered on the way if there could really be any new information awaiting them there.

Backward Progress

"Wouldn't we already have received something at Bunker Hill if it were part of the hunt?" Adam whispered to Ashley. "I mean, wouldn't that be something they passed out the first day?"

Ashley wondered too but didn't want to quit yet. "Who knows?" she said. "It's our last shot, though, at a solution. Keep your fingers crossed."

As they arrived, a ranger from the National Park Service was giving an account of the Battle of Bunker Hill to a group of visitors. Since it was a large group listening, the Arlingtons picked up an information sheet, which featured an essay compiled by Chris Groboske. They waved to the Dunns, who were in the middle of the group, and Mrs. Arlington read quietly to her family:

"The Battle of Bunker Hill started when the colonists learned about the British plan to occupy Dorchester Heights. The colonists felt they had to protect their land and freedom. A crude 'army' was made to defend the hill. This hastily combined force of men had no assigned commander in chief, but did whatever their revered generals instructed them to do.

"On June 15, 1775, the colonists heard that the British planned to control the Charlestown peninsula. Bunker and Breed's Hills on this peninsula overlooked both Boston and its harbor, thus making the hills critical vantage points. In order to beat the British to the high ground, Colonel William Prescott took 1,200 of his oftentimes disobedient soldiers to dig into and fortify Bunker Hill under the cover of night on June 16. When dawn broke, the British were stunned to see Breed's Hill had been fortified overnight with a 160-by–30-foot earthen structure.

"So it was that Colonel Prescott did not actually fortify Bunker Hill, but Breed's Hill instead. How did this happen? One proposed idea is that since they fortified the hill in the middle of the night, Prescott chose the wrong hill. Another theory is that the map he used was incorrect. Another suggestion is that Breed's Hill was closer to where the British ships were positioned, allowing the colonists a better attacking position than at Bunker Hill. Regardless of the reason, the Battle of Bunker Hill actually took place on Breed's Hill.

"The fighting began at daybreak. As soon as the men on the British frigate awoke, they opened fire on the colonial fortifications. They would fire for about twenty minutes, then there would be a lull, then the ships would start firing again. At about 3:00 P.M. Thomas Gage, the British commander, ordered 2,300 men to try and take control of the hill. Peter Brown, an American soldier, would later write about this,

> There was a matter of 40 barges full of Regulars coming over to us; it is supposed there were about 3,000 of them and about 700 of us left not deserted, besides 500 rein-

> forcements . . . the enemy landed and fronted before us and formed themselves in an oblong square . . . and after they were well formed they advanced towards us, but they found a choakly (sic) mouthful of us.

"After the British Regulars established themselves at the base of the hill, they proceeded to charge. According to British letters and diaries, so confident were they that they could just march up the hill and scare the colonists away that many of their muskets were not even loaded. The British 'Red Coats' advanced steadily with their bayonets fixed. The colonists remained calm and held their fire, Colonel Prescott supposedly having given the famous order, 'Don't shoot until you see the whites of their eyes.'

"Twice the colonists drove back the British forces, but on the third attempt the British broke through the tentative American fortifications and took the hill. The colonists fled back up the peninsula, their only escape route. The battle had lasted three hours and was one of the deadliest of the Revolutionary War. Though they had 'won' the hill, the British suffered too many losses to fully benefit from it—more than 1,000 casualties.

"The colonists had suffered perhaps half the casualties, and they felt they had also won in some ways—they had proved to themselves and the world that they could stand up to the British army. Only a few days later, George Washington would, in fact, lead a group of men up to Dorchester Heights, from where they would aim their cannons at the British army and watch the Red Coats retreat from the hill. The colonists would take control of the hill once again, this time with more soldiers to defend it."

In a few minutes, Pete Parnell, the ranger, was finished speaking. The Arlingtons went over to meet the Dunns, and both families introduced themselves to the ranger.

Ashley gave a quick account of what they had been through during the scavenger hunt.

"The last I heard, that had been called off," Pete said.

Adam unzipped his backpack and showed Pete what they had learned.

"This," Pete said, "is bizarre. We received a FedEx package today from England, and it says 'Scavenger Hunt' on it. But it doesn't have a specific return address or name, and shipping was paid for in cash. We are wary of packages like that, so we hadn't opened it. We planned to turn it over to the authorities. I think it's still in the office. Let me check the status and whether it's okay to open it up."

The Arlingtons and Dunns waited for about ten minutes. Soon Pete came out with three other rangers, including the superintendent of the monument.

"Come on into the office," Pete said, introducing the families. "Let's check out the package but not out here."

They went in, and Adam ran down the account they had given Pete a few minutes earlier. The superintendent and the other rangers were very interested.

"Well," said the superintendent, Carol Cann, "I think you kids should open this. We had it x-rayed, and it's nothing dangerous or explosive."

The four kids expressed their appreciation. Ashley took charge, opening the package at one end. There was another wooden bell, like the first one from Arlington, only this one said "Revere" on the side of it.

She handed it to Adam, who turned it upside down. Sure enough, on the bottom were the letters *OC*. He passed it to Ryan and Rachel to see.

There was again a piece of parchment paper, but this time there was no history lesson on the paper. It read:

"If there are twelve letters, you have them all. As you've gone up and down the trail, you've had to go back and forth in history. Sometimes it didn't seem to make sense. But backward makes sense. Your message formed by those twelve letters is your destination. Free the bell a final time. Break the chain. Make things as they a pier, because that's where the answer will ring out."

The park rangers didn't know what was going on, because they didn't have all the clues like the Arlingtons and Dunns did. The kids asked if they could sit. Behind them was a table, and Pete and Carol pulled up seats for them; the four parents politely declined, choosing to stand and see what their kids could come up with using the clues.

The brothers and sisters turned the wooden carvings upside down, lining them up in a row.

"N-O-I-T-U-T-I-T-S-N-O-C," Adam said, writing in a notebook he had taken out of his backpack. "Let's see . . ."

Adam counted the letters.

"Yep, there are twelve," Ryan said.

Ashley looked at the carvings and then at the paper.

"But that word doesn't make any sense," Rachel said.

They stared at it, and Ashley suddenly stood, leaning over the table and pointing at the notebook.

"Backward—we're told that 'backward makes sense,'" Ashley said, referring to the note in the final clue.

She pulled the notebook in front of her and transposed the letters.

"C-O-N-S-T-I-T-U-T-I-O-N . . . it spells Constitution!" they all read at once.

The rangers glanced at each other.

"Good work," Carol Cann said. "I wonder if it means the Constitution as in the document or as in the ship?"

Mr. Arlington scratched his chin. "That's a good question," he said. "Both played key roles in history. Certainly, the document has much more meaning to the country and to the world. But in Boston, the ship certainly has an aura and meaning all its own."

Everybody agreed with that statement. Adam stood, pointing to the note.

"That reference to 'pier'—we've come back to it again and again," he said. "That tells me that this is pointing to the USS *Constitution*. Only that *Constitution* has a pier by it. But what could be there? We've already visited there."

Things started to fall into place for Ashley.

"Would it be on the pier, and not on the ship this time?" Ashley asked. "I don't know if this sounds silly to you, but the one-of-a-kind clue said 'Take the plunge,' remember? And now we have this reference to breaking the chain . . . could there be something attached to the pier by a chain?"

"I don't know, but how can we rule it out without checking?" Rachel asked.

Remembering what she had read online the night before as she tried to learn more about Paul Revere, Ashley connected two other facts. "This wooden carving is of a bell, and it says 'Revere' on it," she said. "Paul Revere's blacksmith shop made bells. Hold on, I have it here . . ."

She took her notebook out of her purse and flipped through the pages.

"Here it is," Ashley said. "I made some notes last night reading the web site. Paul Revere 'supplied brass fittings for the USS *Constitution,* produced cannons, and after 1792, cast bells. One of his largest bells still rings in Boston's King's Chapel.'"

The rangers and the kids' parents thought those might be connected.

"It could mean something," Pete said. "That's too many coincidences to be just a shot in the dark, what with the bell, Revere, the ship, and so on."

Adam started to organize the Arlingtons' carvings and notes, putting them back in sealed plastic bags.

"I think that we're going to have to head back to the ship, then," Ashley said. The three other teens agreed.

Mrs. Arlington raised her hand slowly. "I'm not sure that next step is for us," she said.

Adam zipped his backpack and turned toward his mother. "Why not, Mom?" he asked. "We could be on the verge of solving this thing."

His parents didn't say a word to each other, but both were thinking the same thing.

"You two have done an outstanding job," their father said. "But the USS *Constitution* is run by the United States Navy. And several of the other Freedom Trail stops are run by the National Park Service, including the one here at Bunker Hill. I think if there is anything to be uncovered, it would be the right of the Park Service and Navy to pursue it. They're not going to let just anyone dive into the water around the *Constitution.* I'm sure there are security concerns. We certainly didn't suspect this scavenger hunt would lead in this direction. But, now that it has, we have an obligation to let it move forward in the proper manner."

Carol Cann and Mr. and Mrs. Dunn nodded.

"Thank you, Anne and Alex, Lawrence and Kathleen—and especially you four kids for bringing this not just to our attention but bringing the scavenger hunt along. Big or small, it's definitely worth pursuing. Let me call over to the ship and see what they think," Carol said. "I don't know if the Navy even wants us involved. But we'd like to be, and we'll offer our services if needed."

Adam handed the wooden carvings, the notes, and everything from the search to Pete.

"Listen, kids," Pete said, speaking quietly because Carol had reached the ship on the telephone and had been transferred to the closest Navy base, "we'll keep you posted."

Since it was obvious Carol needed some privacy, the Arlingtons and Dunns headed out of the office.

"Let's go wait outside," Mr. Dunn said. He looked at Pete. "Here's our cell phone number. We'll all be eating dinner together if you need to reach us."

Pete understood. "I told the kids that we're going to call you just as soon as we know anything," he said. "Those four have earned the right to be informed—and I hope included—as this thing draws to a close. I think this scavenger hunt turned up more than anyone ever thought it could—though we don't know for certain at this point."

"Okay," Mr. Dunn told him. "We'll be hoping for your call." He turned to his family and the Arlingtons. "It's still a little early for dinner. Let's go somewhere to have some tea and talk? We can order dinner when we're ready."

Adam and Ashley weren't as upset as their parents thought they would be heading to the car. Their dad asked if they were all right.

"I think everything is going to be fine," Ashley said. "Sure, we wanted to see this through. And given a choice, we probably would have wanted to resolve it on our own. But sometimes that's just not how the world works. It was the right thing to turn it over to the Navy and the National Park Service. We're not even Bostonians. We're guests in this town. That we could help means a lot in itself."

Mr. Arlington glanced proudly at his wife.

"That's a very mature attitude," he said, starting the car and heading to the restaurant. "I think both your mother and I wanted to see you kids finish this thing off. At the same time, there's a right way to do it and a wrong way. I'm glad you kids took the high road."

Adam wasn't his usual talkative self, but he knew the point his father and sister had made was correct.

"We just put in so much work," Adam said. "It kind of seemed, at first, unfair that we couldn't see the hunt through its final stage. But I suppose it's like a baseball game, where a starting pitcher goes eight of the nine innings, and his team is winning when he's pulled out of the game. Someone else comes in and finishes the job. And even though the starting pitcher is on the bench by then, he's still a part of the win because he's the one who helped put his team in a position to win."

Adam's mom was impressed. "That's a pretty accurate analogy," she told him.

As the Arlingtons met the Dunns in the lobby of the restaurant they had chosen, Mr. Dunn's cell phone began to ring. He picked it up and nodded his head a few times as a huge grin spread across his face.

"Thank you! Thank you very much!" he said into the phone, then hung up. "That was Carol Cann, the superintendent we all met at Bunker Hill," he told the group. "She says we're supposed to be at the USS *Constitution* at 7 P.M. tonight, but that we're not to spread that around. The Navy and Park Service are meeting together this afternoon at a military base to coordinate their efforts. Tonight they are going to join forces down at the ship. It's not going to be open to the public, but they want us there!"

Adam looked in his notebook. "That's an hour after closing time!" he noted. "That must mean they think something is really there!"

Ashley realized the importance of the timing.

"And by doing it after closing time, they can have some privacy," she figured. "Maybe they'll even mark off the area so as not to attract a crowd." She glanced at her parents, who seemed deep in thought.

"Will you let us know what happens?" she asked Rachel and the rest of the Dunns. "By 7:00 we'll probably be on our way to eating Dad's lobster on Cape Cod."

"Of course—you can count on it. We have each other's home phones and e-mail addresses," said Rachel. "I can't wait to see what it is they think they'll find, and I'll let you know everything that happens."

Mr. Arlington smiled at his daughter and gave a mock sigh. "I guess those lobsters are just going to have to wait for me one more night," he said. "We've seen the scavenger hunt through this far—we can't jump ship now!"

Stepping off the Trail

"Yes!" Adam and Ashley exclaimed together. Ashley even gave her dad a hug, while Mrs. Arlington put an arm around Adam's shoulder.

"Looks like we're still in the ball game," Mrs. Arlington said with a gentle squeeze of Adam's shoulder. "Whatever happens now is out of our hands, but no matter what it is, we can be there to see it. You four kids have handled your role in this extremely well!"

Mr. and Mrs. Dunn heartily agreed. The two families then took a large table outside the restaurant, ordered cool drinks, and asked for dinner menus.

"This would be a good time to call Jason Jackson at the leadership camp," Mr. Arlington suggested. "He did ask us to keep him apprised of any developments, and though he never expected us to get this far with the scavenger hunt—we never expected to get this far ourselves—we had better let him in on this. After all, the leadership camp was the source of this whole thing."

"Right," Mr. Dunn agreed. He handed over his cell phone so Mr. Arlington could make the call.

"You did *what?*" Jackson said incredulously when he heard Mr. Arlington's news. "Unbelievable!"

Mr. Arlington filled Jackson in on the details of the hunt so far. He suggested he might want to see what—if anything—turned up down at the pier at 7:00. "You should probably come alone and go in with us, though," he told Jackson. "The Park Service told us it's a private situation."

"I'll be there—you can count on it!" Jackson told him. "We've been talking about your 'hopeless hunt' in the camp office. No one thought anything would come of it, even with Adam and Ashley Arlington and Rachel and Ryan Dunn on the trail—though all the staff agreed that if anyone could pull it off, it would be those two sets of siblings. They're some of the best leadership material we've had come through the camp in a long time! But I just can't believe they've actually brought the hunt to this point!"

"I appreciate your words," Mr. Arlington told Jackson. "They are a special group of kids," he said, winking at the teens around the table. "And we'll meet you in the USS *Constitution*'s parking lot at 7:00 tonight."

Mr. Arlington hung up. "I'd say he was a little amazed at the progress you kids have made on what the camp staff has been calling a 'hopeless hunt,'" he told the others. "We'll see him down at the pier tonight."

"We have some time to kill before heading back to the pier," Mrs. Arlington said, sipping her iced tea. "We always like to review what we've learned from a vacation or adventure together," she told the Dunn family. "Would you like to do that with us?" she asked the Dunns. "Any way you look at it, this will probably be our good-bye meal—and we've enjoyed every one of them and every minute we've spent getting to know your family!"

"That sounds great—sometimes we do the same thing," Mrs. Dunn replied. "I hate to think of this as our last time eating together, but you're right. After the excitement of tonight—whatever that turns out to be—you'll no doubt be off to the Cape. So yes, let's talk now about what it has meant to all of us and what lessons we can take home with us."

"What did you kids learn from this adventure, then?" Mrs. Arlington asked, turning to all four teens.

Ashley offered to go first. "I think Dad's 'save' is something I need to remember," she said. "When he gave our number to Petty Officer Kuhl, he saved the scavenger hunt—kept it alive. Chalk one up to 'Sherlock Dad' for quick thinking! I hope I can be like that when situations seem impossible or hopeless in the future.

"But I also learned a lot about leadership," she added. "So many patriots sacrificed so much for independence. They laid the foundation for our country for the next 200 years and beyond."

"That's right," Rachel spoke up. "We learned at leadership camp to think not just of the moment, but of all the moments to come when making an important leadership decision—remember, Ashley?"

Ashley, Adam, and Ryan nodded.

"Who knows what would have happened if the colonists had not had the courage to push for independence?" Rachel continued. "We might not be sitting here like this now. They were outnumbered in troops and resources, but carried on in sheer determination, I think."

Adam went next.

"For me, the history and leadership lessons were important too," he said. "But the bigger thing about the adventure is the journey. I'm curious to know how this is going to turn out. We don't know if our work is going to actually lead to anything, but the journey is what means the most.

"Of course, this was a hands-on history lesson at every stop. No matter how it turns out, we learned a lot about the history of our country's beginnings, especially in the Boston area. We could have just focused on getting the clues and bypassed the places that didn't have clues. Instead, we stopped to find out what led to the independence and liberties we have today. That means a lot."

"It sure does," Ryan said. "I think one of America's greatest strengths is the variety of leaders back then. Samuel Adams was very loud in the way he led—like I can be—and he was always pushing for the colonists' rights. John Hancock was a great thinker—like Rachel is—able to organize his thoughts and put them into words. George Washington was the ultimate warrior. And Crispus Attucks is one of my favorites. He and the other slaves were brought to America for all the wrong reasons, yet he turned it around, and he and other former slaves became leaders too for independence."

"That is amazing," Mrs. Arlington said. "Crispus Attucks and the other slaves took what was a very negative beginning for them and turned it into being able to become proud, important members of the colonies. I think without the direction provided by so many great and diverse leaders, liberty may not have come for America until years, maybe decades, later—if it ever came at all."

There was little doubt that thought was true.

"How can you all apply this when we get home?" Mrs. Dunn prompted this time.

Ashley again decided to answer first.

"I think leading by example is the most important thing," she said. "A few years ago, I was the tallest girl on the volleyball team, and the best player. But in the last year or two, some of the girls improved a lot and became better players than I am. Still, I was able to remain a team leader by working as hard as ever and always offering encouragement. That's what you did for our team on the camp-out assignment, Rachel, and it really works. Coach said one of the things she likes about me is that I can always 'keep the team on the same page.' You don't always have to be the biggest or strongest or smartest to be a good leader. You just have to know your role, where you fit in, like Samuel Adams, Patrick Henry, and Paul Revere did."

"Speaking of the camp-out assignment," Rachel said, "I learned something good from that to apply after I get home. The other team's leader—the 'loud' guy"—she nudged Ryan, who scowled—"acted like he knew everything about everything, and I think he bluffed it even when he didn't know just to psyche our team out. But we kept at our tasks, helping each other and working together, and our team ended up having more success than the one Ryan was on, even if our leader—me—was more low-key and less knowledgeable about camping. We used the talents every team member had. For example, I put Ashley and Adam in charge of setting up the tents because they were experts at that, and we pulled ahead of the other team. It's like the story of the tortoise and the hare. The hare may already look like the winner at the start, but at the finish it can be a whole different story!"

"Good work!" Mr. Dunn commented. "You sure don't have to be loud and rough-and-tumble—even though it seems to be the style your brother and I prefer—to be a great leader. Look at your mother. She's low-key and quiet too, but she rules this family with an iron hand!"

Everyone thought that was funny, but Mr. Dunn assured them it was also true.

Adam also had an idea. "I think if I apply what I've learned about leadership, I can get the lunchroom menu improved!" he said.

Mr. Arlington was taken aback.

"No midnight horseback rides through the school campus, and no cannonballs though, right?" he jokingly asked.

"Of course not, Dad," Adam answered. "But maybe if we get together a good presentation of what we'd like to see, and if we present it in the right way, we can get something we've wanted for a long time—and get freedom from some of the food we've been suffering under!"

"I hear you there!" Ryan said. "Sometimes it seems like we're in permanent bondage to our school cook—you think yours is bad, you should come visit and try ours!"

"Maybe you could try my idea at your school too, then," Adam said to Ryan.

It was too early to tell if Independence Day would come for Adam's and Ryan's lunch concerns, but the sentiment seemed worthwhile.

"Okay, your turn, parents," Ashley said. "Were there things we could have done better to make this hunt possibly more successful?"

"That's a loaded question!" Mr. Dunn commented. "Do your teens always ask for such important advice?" he asked the Arlingtons in amazement.

"Oh, they didn't used to," Mr. Arlington laughed back, "but now that they know we're going to tell them what we think anyway, they figure they might as well ask away and get it over with sooner rather than later."

"Dad!" Ashley protested. "That's not true. We always think your advice is valuable and important."

"Well, almost always," Adam added under his breath, bringing a hearty laugh from Mr. Dunn.

"Since you're so ready for our advice, I'll go first," Mrs. Arlington said, smiling. "You kids approached this with great passion," she said. "Passion is a good thing. But it has to be guided in the right direction. There were a couple of times when our two didn't want to call it a day. There came a point where these places were shutting down. Had you rushed to the remaining places you wanted to visit, you might've come across as pushy, or even come across as rushing people because time wasn't going to permit as full and detailed a search as you were hoping for. Plus, it was getting so late in the day that you kids were getting worn down. You have to keep those things in mind."

"That happened with our two as well," Mrs. Dunn said.

Then it was Mr. Arlington's turn.

"I think we get caught up looking at the little picture, and lose sight of the big picture," he said. "In that regard, Adam and Ashley, you two did a very good job most of the time. You knew that each stop was important to put together all of these pieces to the puzzle. A puzzle is a funny thing, because when your face is right down against it as you gather pieces, you don't get a clear vision of what is being built. Then, after you have the pieces in place for a while and you step back, you get a much better picture of what you've built, or are building. I think that's why we never thought to assemble the letters backward until the very end. We were so caught up in getting to the next wooden carving that we never considered the letters being put together in a different way to make sense.

"Does that mean that we could have solved the thing sooner and spelled Constitution earlier? Maybe. Maybe not. However, had we ever been unable to get a clue along the way—and there were a few times that that almost happened—we would have been better served to look at the clues we did have from a different angle. Had we been missing a couple of letters, we might still have been able to figure out the word 'Constitution.' The important thing is to never lose sight of the big picture, and to remember that the little pictures are all part of that."

Mr. Dunn also had some thoughts on that.

"Like you said, Alex, every piece of the puzzle is important, and sometimes you can overlook a piece if you're going about things too fast. At times I realized, Rachel and Ryan, that our family was going along the Freedom Trail too fast because we wanted to catch up to the Arlingtons—even though it was only by a few minutes or by maybe one stop. Had we been going that fast on the scavenger hunt alone or without them paving the way in front, we might easily have missed a clue. We need to be careful not to let a spirit of competition ruin a spirit of diligence and thoroughness. I'm not saying that it was a big problem—just one to be cautious of in the future."

The Arlingtons and Dunns continued to talk about the kids' leadership camp and all the events surrounding the scavenger hunt as they ordered and ate their dinner. Before they knew it, it was time to drive back to the USS *Constitution* for the unveiling of whatever mysterious reward awaited the successful scavenger hunters—provided it would actually be found.

As the two families parked their cars, they saw Jason Jackson had already arrived and was waiting for them.

"Congratulations," he said, approaching and shaking hands with the four teens and their parents. "We at the camp are amazed—and very pleased—that you kids have brought to this point what we'd already given up on. I can't wait to see what happens next!"

"Let's go, then," said Ryan excitedly.

They all laughed and walked quickly toward the pier. At the entrance they saw police tape marking off the area.

"I'm sorry, folks," said a policeman who stopped them. "The USS *Constitution* is closed for the night."

Mr. Arlington introduced himself and his family, the Dunns, and Mr. Jackson. "We're supposed to be down here after hours," he told the policeman.

"I've heard of your leadership camp. You do good work with kids!" the policeman said, turning to Mr. Jackson.

Mr. Jackson explained to the officer about the canceled scavenger hunt and how because of the kids it had progressed to a possible retrieval of something at the pier.

"I knew there was something big going on down there, what with all the officials showing up and the area being cordoned off. It sounds like you've had a big part in it already, but you'll have to read the rest in the newspaper—I still have to keep everyone out," the policeman said.

The policeman was joined by another officer.

"I'm sorry," the new officer restated, "but we're going to have to ask your group to leave. We have specific instructions that *no one* is to enter the area."

Both officers turned away.

"Excuse me!" Mr. Dunn called after them in his booming voice. "If you'll just talk to the Navy officers down there, I think you'll find . . ."

"Sirs, you and your families need to turn around right now," the second policeman said to Mr. Arlington and Mr. Dunn. "If you don't comply with that, we will have to arrest you. This is an off-limits area marked off by the City of Boston and the United States Navy. Sirs, this is not a matter open to negotiation. I apologize for any miscommunication. But you'll have to leave."

The four teens looked at each other in astonishment. They could see lights and activity down by the pier. They were fifteen minutes early, yet it appeared plenty was already going on down by the ship.

"Isn't there anything you can do?" Adam asked Mr. Jackson.

"I'm sorry," Jackson said. "You heard the officer—he knows about our camp's connection to this event, but apparently that doesn't matter right now. And his partner was very clear—they've got orders not to let us through."

"Let's go," Mr. Arlington urged. "We're not going to accomplish anything by aggravating these policemen. We'll head back to the parking lot and see if Mr. Dunn can call Carol Cann or Petty Officer Kuhl on the cell phone."

Adam, Ashley, Ryan, and Rachel were crushed, and so were their parents.

"This can't be happening!" Adam cried. "All we worked for is unfolding at the pier right now—without us!"

Freedom Rings Again

As the Arlingtons and Dunns turned to head back to the parking lot, they heard more activity behind them. Still, they knew it wouldn't be a good idea to loiter in a place the police had roped off.

A woman in a Navy uniform was running toward the barrier. "Ashley! Rachel!" She called to the girls first. Then she approached the police officer and told him to get the Arlingtons and Dunns, who were almost out of earshot.

"Sirs, sirs!" the policeman called to the men they had just sent away.

The families stopped and turned around, though by that point they were a good one hundred yards down the road.

"Sirs," the policeman said, "I apologize. I didn't know you were all invited. There's a woman down there at the blockade waiting for you now."

The group walked back toward the ship and saw Petty Officer Kuhl. They greeted her and introduced her to Mr. Jackson, explaining his connection with the leadership camp that set up the scavenger hunt.

"Come on!" she said, grabbing Ashley and Rachel by the hands. "They're going to bring it up!"

Ashley and Rachel looked back toward their parents and brothers.

"Hurry!" Adam said, overhearing Kuhl. "They're going to bring it up!"

"What is 'it'?" Mr. Arlington asked.

"No idea, Dad, just come on!" Ashley said, pulling him along with her free hand. He grabbed his wife's hand too, and both families ran down to the pier.

On the pier were about two dozen people, almost all of them in uniforms from the U.S. Navy and the National Park Service.

"Coming through, Sir!" Kuhl said to an officer near the end of the pier where several uniformed men and women were leaning over the water.

"Get the divers in here as soon as they arrive," said a man, whom Kuhl identified to the families as Commander Leon Leftwitz.

Kuhl explained to the families that the clues they had provided had, in fact, led to what could be some sort of discovery. As she spoke, Pete and Carol Cann from Bunker Hill approached and were smiling.

"Kids, we're not certain yet, but we think we are on to something here," Pete said. "You should have seen the huddling this afternoon, with the military, the Navy, the Boston Historical Society, and even some of the state's politicians involved. The divers will soon arrive and see what's down there."

The teens looked at each other excitedly.

"What's down there? What do you mean?" Ashley asked.

Kuhl explained that they had been in conference all afternoon, putting together the clues along with the facts the families had provided.

"There's a chain around the pier," Kuhl said. "We think that someone sneaked in a week or two ago, and threw something in the water, chaining it to the pier. The chain is slightly below the water line, so we can't get to it that easily. We're exercising caution—until divers come and make sure it's not a destructive device, we're going to wait to raise whatever is down there."

Adam raised his hand.

"You're not in school," Kuhl said, smiling as she patted Adam on the back. "But that's respectful of you, Adam. What are you thinking?"

Adam's guess was based on all the information they had assembled. "It could be something relating to the late 1700s," he said. "Our first clue was about 'Why Freedom Rings,' so that leads me to believe that it is something associated with the War for Independence."

Ashley had a similar thought.

"Or it could be something related to the Constitution," she added. "Either the ship or the document."

Pete laughed. "Let's hope it's not a document," he said, "or it will be illegible by now. Documents would not do well in this water. Of course, if that were the case, I don't know why anyone would toss it in and attach it to a chain. They could've just mailed it."

That perked Rachel's interest. "That's what makes this whole thing so intriguing," she said. "Why a scavenger hunt? Why not just a phone call that something is in there? Why not just a letter or an e-mail?"

Kuhl thought about those questions. "Perhaps it would have been easier to trace that way," Kuhl said. "Though this was a scavenger hunt, there seems to have been little rhyme or reason. And from what Pete filled me in on, you folks almost never got started. Apparently there were problems from the beginning."

The kids and Mr. Jackson nodded.

"Right," Ashley said. "Whoever sent in the material to get everyone started didn't leave an address or phone number. Some complications came up, and the night of the first meeting, the hunt was called off. In fact, along the way we even fished one of the papers out of a trash can."

Still, everyone was assembled here now and glad for it. And no one would likely have been gathered that evening had it not been for the Arlingtons and Dunns.

"Adam, Ashley, Rachel, and Ryan, we met with the military people and historical officials this afternoon. The notes and clues you shared with us today really brought us to this point. There *is* something down there. We didn't come down until the ship was closed for the day—we didn't want this to turn into a big circus. Well, as one thing led to another, we ended up roping off the area, and the police were instructed to let no one in."

Ashley smiled. "Yes, we noticed," she said, recounting how they were thrown off the property under threat of arrest.

"I'm sorry," Carol said. "That's certainly an irony, isn't it? You kids get us here, and then you almost didn't get to see how this turns out. We still don't know what's down there. But we're here because of you."

Petty Officer Kuhl agreed that was the case.

"I had no idea when you kids approached me that it would lead to anything," Kuhl said. "I mean, a scavenger hunt that no one—save two very special families—participates in—what's that all about? However, had you not gone after this with such vigilance, we wouldn't be here talking right now."

A large van pulled up, and two people dressed in Navy uniforms emerged at the top of the hill. Out of the back of the van came two Navy divers, already in wet suits.

"That's them!" Kuhl said. "Well, pretty soon we could have an answer. I know it's too late to tell anyone not to get their hopes up. But, really, we have no reason to be either optimistic or pessimistic."

Adam and Ashley smiled.

"We already had that talk from our parents," Ashley said. "Either way though, at least we might get some closure on this thing. No matter what happens, it sure has been a lot of fun. It was educational, too. I already know what I'm doing my term paper on for history this fall—Boston and the Freedom Trail."

"And I have a great adventure story to write up for my school newspaper," Rachel added.

Carol and Pete stood up, and the group followed suit.

"Sounds like you all made the most of this," Carol said. "And that you did it basically from scratch says a lot about your perseverance."

Everyone was told to move back off the pier except for a couple of Navy officials and the divers. After putting on masks and oxygen tanks, the divers received final instructions from Leftwitz. Though they were off the pier, the Arlingtons, Dunns, Jackson, Kuhl, Pete, and Carol could hear his directions to the divers, a woman and a man.

"The chain is around the pier," Leftwitz said. "We don't know what is at the end of the chain. If you two think anything is amiss, let me know right away. We could get a bomb squad in or even shut down the whole area and bring in a submersible tomorrow morning if need be. Err on the side of caution, no matter what."

The divers said they understood and decided to go in on opposite sides of the pier. A large light was lowered into the water, and both divers also took large underwater flashlights with them. They slipped into the water, and Leftwitz put in an earpiece. Kuhl explained to the families that it would allow the divers to communicate with Leftwitz. The divers were down for about eight minutes. Leftwitz pulled the plug from his ear.

"All right, everyone, we're clear of any danger," he said. "You can come back down here now."

Kuhl led the families to the edge of the pier and introduced the teens to Leftwitz.

"Sir, these young people are the reason we're here," Kuhl said. "They're the ones who provided the notes and clues that we combed through this afternoon at the base."

Leftwitz shook their hands. "Thanks for the detective work," he said. "You showed a lot of determination."

As he spoke, the divers started to surface. One was holding the chain, coiling it in as the other diver brought up a black object perhaps a foot high and eighteen inches wide. As they broke through the water, Leftwitz instructed Petty Officer Kuhl to carefully retrieve the object.

Kuhl grabbed at what appeared to be a poncho.

"It's heavy," said the male diver. "I'll need some help."

The woman diver clipped the chain from the pier and handed that up. She then helped the other diver push the object up. As it came out of the water, the brother and sister duos finally saw it in the light.

"It's in the shape of a bell!" Adam said.

Kuhl and Leftwitz took the object and removed the waterproof poncho from it; it was indeed a cast-iron bell.

"What do you know?" Mr. Arlington whispered to his wife. "The kids were right on the money."

The bell was old but looked rugged. There were chips out of it, but everyone could see some lettering very clearly etched on the side. Kuhl whispered something to Leftwitz, and after he nodded and said, "Sure, that sounds all right," she motioned to Adam, Ashley, Rachel, and Ryan.

"Why don't you four take a look at it?" she said.

The teens were ecstatic, but sensing the aura of professionalism, hid their glee behind four very wide smiles.

Adam gently turned the bell. "Look," he said. "On the side it says, 'Revere.'"

Indeed it did. The letters were well weathered but still plainly readable. The bell might have had a couple of centuries behind it, but the durable iron hadn't yielded much to the years in terms of quality. As Adam turned it a second time, the bell even made a small noise.

"It's obviously in working condition," Kuhl observed.

Just then, one of the divers sat down on the edge of the pier and looked over her shoulder, motioning toward Leftwitz. "Hold on a minute," she said. "Something in a plastic bag slipped out of it. It appears to be weighted, so I'm going to go in after it."

"With caution!" Leftwitz said.

The woman was underwater for several minutes. She descended to the lower-most reaches of the light, then stopped and turned, tucking the flashlight under her arm and holding something in her hand.

She came up to the surface with a letter in an envelope that was packed inside an airtight, clear plastic bag. She handed it to Kuhl, who promptly handed it to Leftwitz. He examined it. Determining there was no hazard or danger, he opened it and read the letter. He handed it to Kuhl.

"Let the kids read it to everyone," he whispered to her.

"Yes, Sir," she answered. She handed it to Ashley.

"Think it's all right if I read it, or do one of you want to?" Ashley quietly asked the others.

"Go ahead," Ryan said. "I want to check out the bell."

Rachel and Adam nodded.

The bell was heavy. Adam guessed that it weighed at least forty pounds.

Ashley opened the envelope, and everyone on the pier listened as she read the letter:

> I have no idea if anyone will find this, but if you have, you have obviously reached the reward. This bell came to me under very poor circumstances. It was taken more than 200 years ago by a relative of mine, who was in the British army and served valiantly in the war against the colonies. From the information passed down in our family, this bell was made by Paul Revere himself.
>
> Was this bell intended for a ship or for another proud historic site in Boston? We don't know. However, as it was passed down through the generations, my family realized that it would have much greater value to the City of Boston than to us. We didn't want to come forward publicly because of the circumstances under which it came into our possession. While it holds meaning to us in that it was brought to our homeland in England by a relative, we know that the rightful owners are among the descendants of the colonists in America and in Boston.
>
> Since I was completing a two-year business assignment in the United States, my grandmother entrusted me with returning the bell to the rightful owners. We wanted resentment from neither side of the ocean, so

we wanted to do it as anonymously as possible. The idea for the scavenger hunt was mine. I contacted a leadership camp group I saw in the paper. It is my hope that the retrievers of this bell will have been enlightened by the history of Boston, a history that should never be forgotten in this state, and indeed in all the others in the United States.

I wish I had found a more honorable way to give this back to you, America. I hope that this is discovered by July 3, so many can enjoy it on Independence Day. Regardless, your bell is now home. Enjoy it. Regards.

Ashley folded the paper. "That's the end of the note," she said. "We're a week early. But with the extra time, maybe something can be put together so a much larger group can 'enjoy it' on Independence Day."

Everyone started clapping.

"It's a great day for Boston—a great day for America," Leftwitz spoke next. "A piece of history has been brought home. Thank you, Adam and Ashley Arlington and Ryan and Rachel Dunn, and your parents as well. I'm sure this will add a great deal to our annual Independence Day celebration. No doubt a lot of media attention will be given to this. And it makes sense to me that this will add an extra helping of patriotic feeling to a holiday that truly holds special meaning here in Boston."

The question facing everyone was what would now happen to the bell.

"One could probably make a good case that the Arlingtons and/or the Dunns could lay claim to this because they did the legwork. And after all, according to the leadership camp's original plan, the special Independence Day reward was supposed to go to the scavenger hunt winners. On the other hand, the overseas donor seemed to intend the bell to ring again for Boston," Kuhl said to the crowd. "I'd like to get some input on this—Mr. and Mrs. Arlington and Mr. and Mrs. Dunn, front and center please."

The Arlington and Dunn adults held a quick conference, then pointed to their kids.

"I think we know what needs to be done here," Adam whispered to the others before Kuhl called them forward.

"Right," Rachel said. "Ashley, go ahead and tell them!"

Ashley smiled and gave Rachel a hug and Ryan and Adam a pat on the back. "C'mon, let's go," she told them.

The four teens stood up and approached Petty Officer Kuhl at the front of the gathering.

"To even be a part of this is something we could never have imagined," Ashley told everyone. "To try and pass off this bell as ours would be unthinkable. We give up any claim whatsoever to it and just ask that the Navy, Park Service, and Boston Historical Society find a proper place for it. We hope everyone who visits Boston finds at least a sliver as much happiness and pride from this bell as we have been blessed to receive as its discoverers."

Leftwitz and Kuhl stepped forward.

"Could you hand us the bell?" Leftwitz asked the four teens, in a symbolic gesture.

Photographers from the Park Service and Navy stepped forward and snapped pictures as Adam, Ashley, Rachel, and Ryan proudly handed the bell to Leftwitz. He brought up officials from the Park Service and the historical society.

"After we inspect this—I'd say within the hour—we'll gladly pass it along to you folks at the Park Service and the historical society to decide where this living piece of history belongs," Leftwitz said. "Certainly this doesn't belong to the U.S. Navy. We're humbled to be involved in getting this item to its rightful place. But that's for you folks at the Park Service and Boston Historical Society, not us. I am sure we can all agree to have it in some sort of special display on the Freedom Trail for July Fourth."

Carol Cann turned toward Mr. and Mrs. Arlington and Mr. and Mrs. Dunn. "You will be here for the Fourth of July, won't you?" she asked.

Mr. Arlington pursed his lips together and shook his head. "I'm afraid we won't," he said. "While this did wrap up a week ahead of the scavenger hunt's prescribed date, we have commitments. We'll be returning home in the next three days—and two of those will be spent on Cape Cod eating seafood and visiting friends. The Cape Cod part of the trip was actually supposed to last a week."

All the Arlingtons laughed. Adam explained how his father had planned the family's trip and had scheduled several days for his favorite part of New England.

"We'll still get down there," Mrs. Arlington said. "To be able to be a part of this was well worth adjusting our original plans. Under any other circumstance, we'd make further adjustments to be here for the Fourth of July. That sounds like a special time, and perhaps more so this year with the bell and everything that will surround the publicity of its discovery and welcome home. But the kids and I have volunteered to work for a parade back home in D.C. on the Fourth. While we are flattered by your invitation, we must respectfully decline because of prior commitments."

Kuhl turned to the Dunns and asked about their plans.

"Actually, we will be staying on in Boston for the Independence Day activities," Mrs. Dunn told her. "We'd be delighted to see the bell's new display when it's ready, and we'll take personal responsibility to see that Anne and Alex and their wonderful kids feel a part of it too—we'll send pictures and also report everything that goes on to them."

"Fantastic!" Ashley told their friends. "We already know what a great reporter Rachel is."

"That'll be terrific—almost as good as being here ourselves," Adam agreed.

"How were you involved?" Kuhl asked Mr. Jackson.

"First just let me say that as our leadership camp's spokesperson, I absolutely agree that this bell should belong to the city of Boston, and I'm so proud of these four kids for recognizing that," he told her. "I'm also absolutely sure that our camp would like to be represented when the bell is put on display. Let us know what the plans are, and I'll be there myself. Right now, though, I'm going to head back to camp and let the rest of the staff in on this discovery!"

Mr. Jackson shook hands with Petty Officer Kuhl and the kids' parents and congratulated Ashley, Adam, Rachel, and Ryan one more time before leaving.

"I hope you'll come back to camp again," he called to them as he walked away. "The four of you are welcome to be junior staff assistants next time!"

The divers and several of the other Navy officials came up to congratulate the kids and their parents, then headed out. Carol and Pete stayed to examine the bell in more detail, as did officials from the Boston Historical Society.

"Certainly this will belong to the historical society," Carol said. "But maybe we can display it along the Freedom Trail in an appropriate location."

Kuhl went and grabbed her duffel bag. From it she took the wooden carvings and the notes.

"At least we know for sure that these are yours," she said, handing them to the teens. "Commander Leftwitz agreed that these are rightfully yours to keep."

The kids were happy to accept them. But then they realized something.

"Actually," Adam said, "this final clue, the wooden carving of a bell with 'Revere' on it, is a match to the bell that was just brought up out of the water. We would like to donate this—and all of the clues from the hunt, including the parchment papers with the notes and the other wooden carvings—to the Park Service and the Boston Historical Society. The British donor took a lot of time to put this scavenger hunt together. It seems only appropriate that these go with the actual bell."

They handed the materials back to Carol.

"Whether the Park Service or historical society takes charge of the bell, it makes sense that these would go along with the display to tell the story behind how we came across this cast-iron piece of history," Carol said. She turned to the crowd and added, "I think we all owe the Arlington and Dunn families a big thank-you for their efforts, and thanks also to the U.S. Navy, the City of Boston Police, and everyone else who helped bring this scavenger hunt to its exciting, heartwarming conclusion."

The small crowd of onlookers clapped loudly as Adam and Ashley went over to their parents and hugged them.

"Thanks so much for letting us follow through on all this," Ashley said. "We know you two sacrificed most of the Cape Cod trip—and a lot of time and energy—to see this through."

Adam agreed. "This has been so much fun, and it opened our eyes to a lot of history," he said. "What a great experience! It would have been great even if we didn't find the bell."

Mr. and Mrs. Arlington looked at their kids.

"But it sure was great that we did find it!" Adam proclaimed, drawing laughs.

Mr. Arlington reached into his pocket and grabbed the keys to the car. "If we hurry, we could reach Cape Cod before midnight!" he said.

Adam and Ashley laughed, knowing their father was playfully poking fun at the way Adam and Ashley had wanted to stay on the go at all costs during the hunt for the bell. It was too late now to start the drive; they'd leave first thing in the morning.

"We'll still get out there," Mr. Arlington added. "Just the thought of seafood at my favorite restaurant on the Cape is making my stomach growl right now."

The Arlington family exchanged handshakes with the crowd and hugs with the Dunn family. Adam took his notebook from his backpack and wrote his and Ashley's e-mail and street addresses down. The Dunns already had the information, but Adam also gave copies to Kuhl, Pete, Carol, and even Commander Leftwitz.

"You see, Dad?" Adam said, "I can be taught."

"That's good," Mr. Arlington said. "And I'd speculate that you will hear from these folks down the line."

Kuhl said she'd keep them updated. "I'm counting on you two to come back and visit the bell—and visit all of us as well," she said.

Pete and Carol said they too would stay in touch, and the Arlingtons said good-bye to everyone and headed back up the hill. After stopping to grab water, a few magazines, and a newspaper, they headed back to their hotel.

By the time they reached the hotel, a couple of television crews and newspaper reporters were on hand, wanting to interview them about their discovery.

"We're going on live for the news," said one station's reporter. "Who will serve as spokesperson for the family?"

Ashley motioned to Adam, and both parents concurred.

"We need to keep it short, though," Mrs. Arlington told the reporters. "We have a long drive ahead of us. We all feel very humbled and very blessed to be associated with not only the bell itself, but all the outstanding people who provided direction and even friendship in this process."

Adam was set up with a microphone, and he briefly recounted the search. "Really, though, we were just two families of tourists who stumbled on to something special," he said. "While the bell is neat and we're glad to have had a part in returning it to Boston, the special thing we stumbled on wasn't the bell itself. The special thing is Boston and all of its history."

He handed the microphone back to the reporter.

"Well stated, young man," the reporter said, patting Adam on the back.

The Arlingtons headed back to their room. They all sat in their suite, talking about the exciting string of events that culminated with the evening's retrieval of the bell.

"For everything that happened and all the excitement," Ashley said, "what I'll remember most are the people we met, especially the Dunns."

That seemed appropriate.

"Me, too," Adam said. "I'll also remember the incredible history lessons we learned. I want to learn even more. So when we get home I'm going to do some more research online and at the library. The history is what I'll never forget. Then again, the history is something no one should ever forget!"

Massachusetts

Fun Fact Files

Arlington Family

Massachusetts

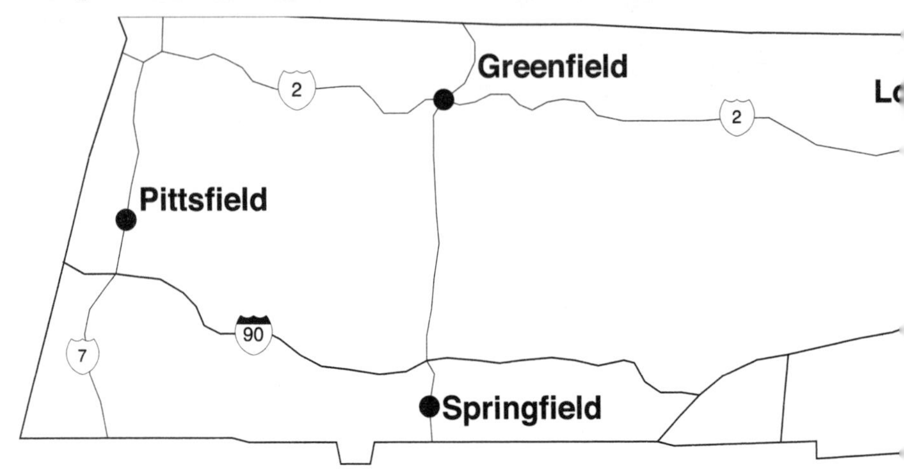

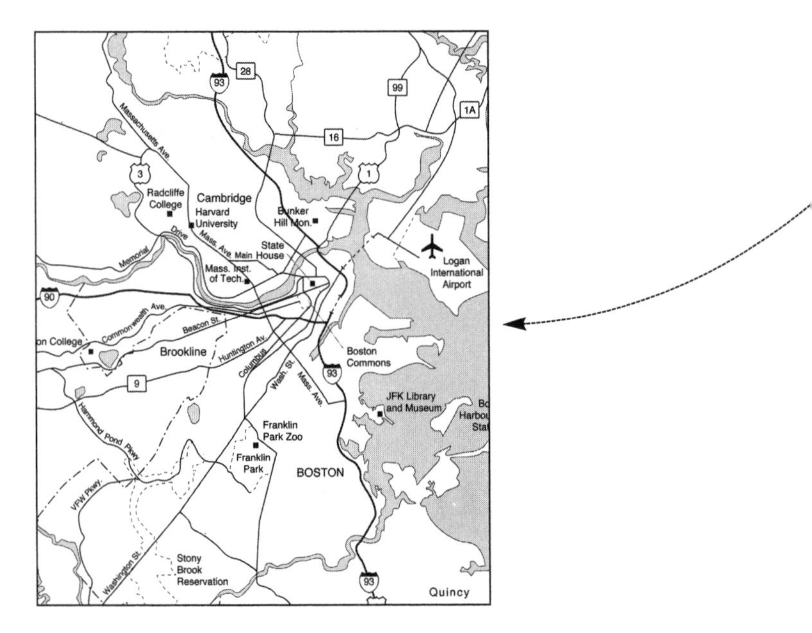

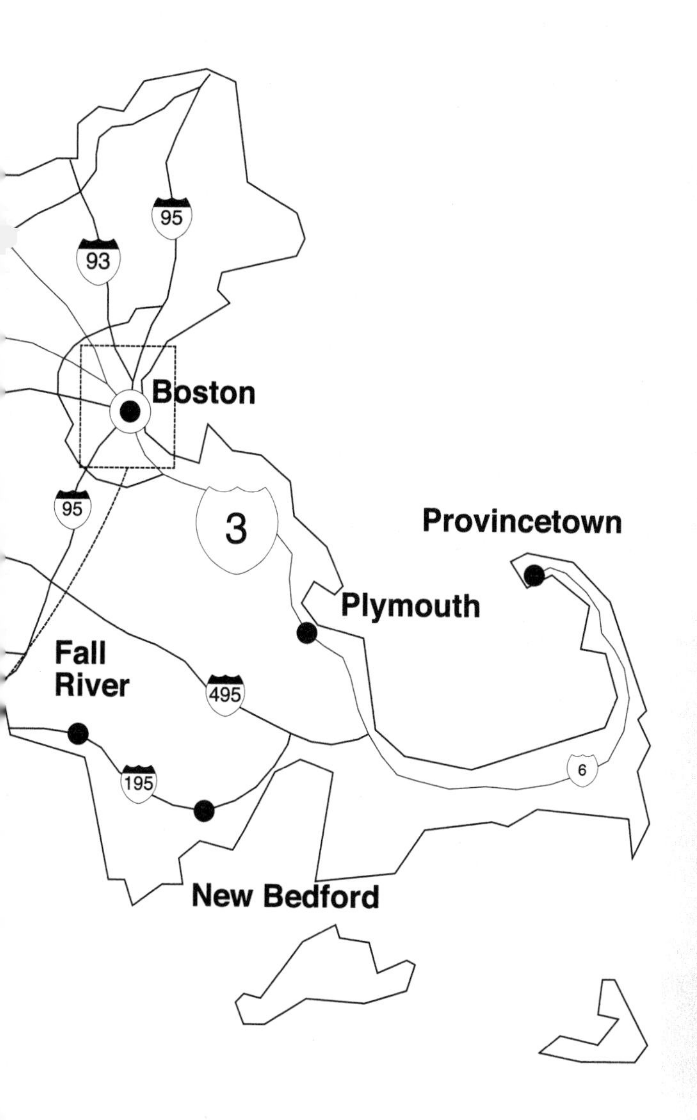

95
93
Boston
95
3
Provincetown
Plymouth
Fall River
495
6
195
New Bedford

Names and Symbols

Origin of Name:

Massachusetts gets its name from the Massachuset tribe of Native Americans that lived in the Great Blue Hill Region south of Boston. The Indian term means "at or about the Great Hill" or "the great mountain."

Nicknames:

The Bay State or The Old Colony State

Motto:

"Ense petit placidam sub libertate quietem" ("By the sword we seek peace, but peace only under liberty")

State Symbols:

flower: mayflower
tree: American elm
bird: black-capped Chickadee
marine mammal: right whale
gemstone: rhodonite
fish: cod
song: "All Hail to Massachusetts"
beverage: cranberry juice

Geography

Location:

New England; Coastal northeastern United States

Borders:

Vermont (North)
New Hampshire (North)
Atlantic Ocean (East)
Rhode Island (South)
Connecticut (South)
New York (West)

Area:

8,284 square miles (6th smallest state)

Highest Elevation:

Mount Greylock (3,491 feet)

Nature

National Parks:

Cape Cod National Seashore
Appalachian National Scenic Trail

Weather

Massachusetts enjoys a temperate climate. The average temperature for July, the hottest month, is 71 degrees Fahrenheit. January is the coldest month with an average temperature of 26 degrees Fahrenheit. The climate varies from east to west within the state—the western part of Massachusetts, away from the coast, tends to be colder but drier and gets more severe snow.

People and Cities

Population: 6,349,097 (2000 census)

Capital: Boston

Ten Largest Cities (1990 census):

Boston (574,283)
Worcester (169,759)
Springfield (156,983)
Lowell (103,439)
New Bedford (99,922)
Cambridge (95,802)
Brockton (92,788)
Fall River (92,703)
Quincy (84,985)
Lynn (81,245)

Counties: 14

Major Industries

Manufacturing:

Massachusetts is an important manufacturing state. Saltworks and ironworks were built very early. In the 1800s, with an influx of unskilled, low-paid laborers from Europe, the state's shoe and textile factories developed methods of mass production. Some well known goods from Massachusetts are watches, rockers, hand tools, paper, and silverware.

Technology:

Today Massachusetts' main industries are technological. The research and development industry has contributed to the advance of computer technology. Electronics and communications industries also continue to grow. These industries are supported by the state's many prestigious educational institutions, among them, Harvard, Tufts, Wellesley, Radcliffe, and Boston University.

Agriculture:

The mostly rocky soil of Massachusetts supports a small farming industry. Greenhouse and nursery products are the main crops, followed by dairy products. The purple sandy bogs of southeastern Massachusetts and Cape Cod yield 50 percent of the United States' cranberry supply—the largest crop in the world. Massachusetts ranks among the top five fishing states in the country.

Tourism:

Massachusetts is famous for its historic buildings, monuments, museums, and libraries. Some of Massachusetts' main resort areas are Cape Cod, Cape Ann, Martha's Vineyard, and Nantucket.

History

Native Americans:

Native Americans arrived in Massachusetts 3,500 years before the Pilgrims landed at Plymouth. The state's original inhabitants include the Nauset, the Massachuset, and the Wampanoag Indian tribes. Although relatively few Native Americans live in Massachusetts today, their presence is echoed in the state's many Indian place names. "Massachusetts" itself is an Indian name. There is even a lake called Lake Chargoggagoggmanchauggagoggchaubunagungamaugg, which means "You Fish on Your Side; I Fish on My Side; Nobody Fishes in the Middle."

Exploration and Settlement:

Leif Eriksson and Norse explorers may have landed on Cape Cod over 1,000 years ago. European fishermen fished the waters off Cape Cod throughout the 1500s. In 1605 French explorer Samuel de Champlain mapped the area. The Pilgrims arrived on the Mayflower during the winter of 1620, and the Puritans came a decade later, in 1630. Both groups were fleeing from religious persecution.

There were originally two colonies within the boundaries of present-day Massachusetts. The Pilgrims founded Plymouth Colony. By the 1640s, the colony had a population of around 3,000. The Puritans settled to the north and founded the Massachusetts Bay Colony. The Massachusetts Bay Colony grew rapidly—the persecution in England worsened steadily, forcing many Puritans to flee to the colonies. By the 1640s, just 10 years after its settlement, over 20,000 people lived in the colony. Massachusetts Bay Colony operated almost like an independent state. It even minted its own money and conducted its own foreign affairs. The king, uncomfortable with the colony's growing sense of independence, revoked its charter in 1684. Later, after revolution in England, the new king and queen issued a new charter to the Province of Massachusetts Bay. The province consisted of Plymouth, Maine, and the islands of Nantucket and Martha's Vineyard. Massachusetts kept this territory until Maine became a separate state in 1820.

Statehood:

entered the union on February 6, 1788 (6th state)

For more information about the historical people and places in this book, check out the following web sites:

Massachusetts:

Web sites:

http://www.state.ma.us/

http://www.50states.com/massachu.htm

The Freedom Trail

Web sites:

http://www.thefreedomtrail.org

http://www.ci.boston.ma.us/freedomtrail/

Bunker Hill

Web site: http://charlestown.ma.us/monument.html

U.S.S. Constitution

Web sites:

http://charlestown.ma.us/constitution.html

http://www.USSconstitution.navy.mil/

Old North Church

Web site: http://www.oldnorth.com/

Boston Massacre

Web site: http://www.bostonmassacre.net/

Boston National Historic Park

Web site: http://www.nps.gov/bost/

Samuel Adams

Web sites:

http://www.samueladams.net/

http://www2.lucidcafe.com/lucidcafe/library/95sep/adams.html

Crispus Attucks

Web site: http://ga.essortment.com/crispusattucks_rhqa.htm

Patrick Henry

Web sites:

http://www.inmind.com/schools/lessons/PatrickHenry/index.html

http://libertyonline.hypermall.com/henry-liberty.html

Paul Revere

Web site: http://www.paulreverehouse.org/